STRING ALONG . . .

with fourteen of the finest, free-swinging reporters of the bestial and bizarre ever to pen a death sentence:

RICHARD HARDWICK
GILBERT RALSTON
AUGUST DERLETH
C. B. GILFORD
JACK RITCHIE
BORDEN DEAL
ROBERT BLOCH
LAURENCE M. JANIFER
FLETCHER FLORA
RICHARD DEMING
JONATHAN CRAIG
ED LACY
DAN J. MARLOWE
HENRY SLESAR

in

ALFRED HITCHCOCK'S
NOOSE REPORT

ALFRED HITCHCOCK'S

NOOSE REPORT

A DELL MYSTERY / AN ORIGINAL VOLUME

Published by
DELL PUBLISHING CO., INC.
750 Third Avenue
New York, N.Y. 10017

First Dell Printing—August, 1966
Printed in U.S.A.

ACKNOWLEDGMENTS

The following stories are reprinted by permission of the authors and the authors' agents, Scott Meredith Literary Agency, Inc.

"HIGH TIDE" by Richard Hardwick—© 1963 by H.S.D. Publications, Inc.

"THE WORLD'S OLDEST MOTIVE" by Laurence M. Janifer—© 1959 by H.S.D. Publications, Inc.

"A VERY CAUTIOUS BOY" by Gilbert Ralston—© 1961 by H.S.D. Publications, Inc.

"SOMETHING VERY SPECIAL" by Fletcher Flora—© 1965 by H.S.D. Publications, Inc.

"OTHERS DEAL IN DEATH" by August Derleth—© 1961 by H.S.D. Publications, Inc.

"THE PROMOTION" by Richard Deming—© 1965 by H.S.D. Publications, Inc.

"CONTENTS: ONE BODY" by C. B. Gilford—© 1963 by H.S.D. Publications, Inc.

"THE LATE UNLAMENTED" by Jonathan Craig—© 1966 by H.S.D. Publications, Inc.

"HOLDOUT" by Jack Ritchie—© 1962 by H.S.D. Publications, Inc. Reprinted by permission of Scott Meredith Literary Agency, Inc. and Larry Sternig Agency.

"THE LITTLE THINGS" by Ed Lacy—©1965 by H.S.D. Publications, Inc. Reprinted by permission of Howard Moorepark Literary Agency.

"MAKE YOUR PITCH" by Borden Deal—© 1962 by H.S.D. Publications, Inc. Reprinted by permission of Paul R. Reynolds, Inc.

"THE SHORT AND SIMPLE ANNALS" *by Dan J. Marlowe*—© 1964 by H.S.D. Publications, Inc. Reprinted by permission of Samuel French, Inc.

"A HOME AWAY FROM HOME" by Robert Bloch—© 1961 by H.S.D. Publications, Inc. Reprinted by permission of Harry Altshuler Literary Agency.

"THE TROUBLE WITH RUTH" by Henry Slesar—© 1957 by H.S.D. Publications, Inc. Reprinted by permission of Theron Raines Literary Agency, Inc.

CONTENTS

INTRODUCTION

by Alfred Hitchcock

IT IS MY SAD DUTY to announce that crime in America, long in a state of decline, has reached a crisis from which recovery looks doubtful. The very foundations of evil are crumbling. The superstructure of sin is tottering. Wickedness is losing ground; depravity is out of the picture; iniquity is done for; turpitude has had it. One must rise early and work feverishly to uncover anything more serious than random naughtiness. The forces of darkness have packed their grips, as it were, and migrated to more hospitable climes. Virtue is in the saddle; the golden age of niceness is upon us.

If the reader disputes these assertions, I need only refer him to the statistics presented to me recently by a contingent of reporters assigned to cover a conference on the subject held at Heavies' Haven, a resort near Appalachin in New York State. The facts, compiled by an independent testing service, speak eloquently in support of my thesis. For example, in 1940 the ratio of nasty people to nice ones was 3 in 10; in 1950, 2.7 in 10; and in 1960, 1.9! Projected for 1970 is the astonishing ratio of three quarters of an unwholesome human for every ten citizens, including servicemen overseas.

Another guideline is ratty behavior. Discounting the Luciano-Dillinger Effect and the Cosa Nostra Compensatory Gradient, we still end up with an average annual decline of 3.6% in rattiness. Similar depreciations can be pointed out in corruption, rottenness, degeneracy and profligacy. Only knavery closed mixed and rascality, for reasons too complicated to go into in this summary, was higher in heavy trading.

The Heavies' Haven conference, after weighing the burden of evidence, turned to the obvious question of what has brought about this sinister turn in the badness movement. Discussion was active, to say the least, and at several points the meetings had to be recessed to allow participants to release hostilities.

Most of the suggestions were dismissed by the group as inadequate. A clever case was made for atomic fallout, and another contributor had the temerity to suggest divine interference as a cause. But no explanation really struck fire among the conferees. However, on the final day a well-dressed gentleman delivered a brief address to his colleagues that brought them roaring to their feet.

"I am a member of the F. B. I.," he said, "and this place is surrounded."

It seems a pity that no worthwhile conclusions were reached by the parley before the members were escorted to a place of detention. However, after reading the minutes and discussing the matter, with the warden's permission, with my reporters, I am able to say confidently that I know what it is that has had such a disturbing effect on the flourishing of crime in our country.

The answer is the Great Society.

As a result of the Great Society, evil has tragically become either unprofitable, dangerous or boring. Money and goods are now so plentiful that one actually must exert all of one's wits to keep from becoming legitimately wealthy. In fact I know of a number of outlaws who work from nine to five keeping America's natural bounty from seeping through the cracks and crannies of their headquarters. Fending off honest income takes up so much of their time that they have to plot foul play during coffee breaks, so you can imagine how effective their schemes turn out to be. When they finally do commit a crime their profit margin is so slim that they would be better off putting their venture capital in a savings bank and reaping a modest interest.

This is assuming their crime is successful. But with modern detection and prevention methods, that assumption is far from a certainty. Thus one reason that the criminal's overhead is so high these days is the cost of detecting detection and preventing prevention. The personnel and equipment required to keep the edge over crime-fighters is truly staggering. Payroll and maintenance devour enormous slices of the evildoer's pie, and administrative and bookkeeping costs drain his capital as fast as he replenishes it. Thus even when he does overcome the danger involved in committing a Modern American Crime, he has laid out of pocket so much front money that a 2% or 3% return is as much as he can expect.

Worst of all is the lack of excitement that characterizes badness these days. There are no interesting people left to kidnap, no novel motives for murder, no breathtaking modes of escape. The hierarchy of the average syndicate consists of an M. A. in Business Administration as the kingpin and a staff of engineers, computer-programmers and tax advisors in the roles of goons, yeggs and plug-uglies. Ties and jackets are *de rigeur* at all antisocial functions, and "please" and "thank you" are common phrases heard in the demanding of loot or ransom.

The next Heavies' Haven Conference will be devoted to revitalizing the flagging evil movement. Papers are now in preparation featuring such titles as "Cutting Operating Expenses through the Eradication of Directors," "One Hundred Burglary Risks You Can Take," "Add Glamor to your Petty Crimes," "Is Nonviolence Here to Stay?" and "Get the Most out of Recent Scientific Developments." Hopefully the forthcoming convention will point the way to restoration of the Power of Black to the throne.

The stories in this album are presented in conjunction with the above-mentioned papers, and represent some of the more promising endeavors towards the goal of rescuing villany from oblivion.

ALFRED J. HITCHCOCK

A HOME AWAY FROM HOME

by Robert Bloch

THE TRAIN was late, and it must have been past nine o'clock when Natalie found herself standing, all alone, on the platform before Hightower Station.

The station itself was obviously closed for the night—it was only a way-stop, really, for there was no town here—and Natalie wasn't quite sure what to do. She had taken it for granted that Dr. Bracegirdle would be on hand to meet her. Before leaving London, she'd sent her uncle a wire giving him the time of her arrival. But since the train had been delayed, perhaps he'd come and gone.

Natalie glanced around uncertainly, then noticed a phone booth which provided her with a solution. Dr. Bracegirdle's last letter was in her purse, and it contained both his address and his phone number. She had fumbled through her bag and found it by the time she walked over to the booth.

Ringing him up proved a bit of a problem; there seemed to be an interminable delay before the operator made the connection, and there was a great deal of buzzing on the line. A glimpse of the hills beyond the station, through the glass wall of the booth, suggested the reason for the difficulty. After all, Natalie reminded herself, this was West Country. Conditions might be a bit primitive—

"Hello, hello!"

The woman's voice came over the line, fairly shouting above the din. There was no buzzing noise now, and the sound in the background suggested a babble of voices all intermingled. Natalie bent forward and spoke directly and distinctly into the mouthpiece.

"This is Natalie Rivers," she said. "Is Dr. Bracegirdle there?"

"Whom did you say was calling?"

"Natalie Rivers. I'm his niece."

"His what, Miss?"

"Niece," Natalie repeated. "May I speak to him, please?"

"Just a moment."

There was a pause, during which the sound of voices in the background seemed amplified, and then Natalie heard the resonant masculine tones, so much easier to separate from the indistinct murmuring.

"Dr. Bracegirdle here. My dear Natalie, this is an unexpected pleasure!"

"Unexpected? But I sent you a 'gram from London this afternoon." Natalie checked herself as she realized the slight edge of impatience which had crept into her voice. "Didn't it arrive?"

"I'm afraid service is not of the best around here," Dr. Bracegirdle told her, with an apologetic chuckle. "No, your wire didn't arrive. But apparently you did." He chuckled again. "Where are you, my dear?"

"At Hightower Station."

"Oh, dear. It's in exactly the opposite direction."

"Opposite direction?"

"From Peterby's. They rang me up just before you called. Some silly nonsense about an appendix—probably nothing but an upset stomach. But I promised to stop round directly, just in case."

"Don't tell me they still call you for general practice?"

"Emergencies, my dear. There aren't many physicians in these parts. Fortunately, there aren't many patients, either." Dr. Bracegirdle started to chuckle, then sobered. "Look now. You say you're at the station. I'll just send Miss Plummer down to fetch you in the wagon. Have you much luggage?"

"Only my travel case. The rest is coming with the household goods, by boat."

"Boat?"

"Didn't I mention it when I wrote?"

"Yes, that's right, you did. Well, no matter. Miss Plummer will be along for you directly."

"I'll be waiting in front of the platform."

"What was that? Speak up, I can hardly hear you."

"I said I'll be waiting in front of the platform."

"Oh." Dr. Bracegirdle chuckled once more. "Bit of a party going on here."

"Shan't I be intruding? I mean, since you weren't expecting me—"

"Not at all! They'll be leaving before long. You wait for Plummer."

The phone clicked off and Natalie returned to the platform. In a surprisingly short time, the station wagon appeared and skidded off the road to halt at the very edge of the tracks. A tall, thin gray-haired woman, wearing a somewhat rumpled white uniform, emerged and beckoned to Natalie.

"Come along, my dear," she called. "Here, I'll just pop this in back." Scooping up the bag, she tossed it into the rear of the wagon. "Now, in with you—and off we go!"

Scarcely waiting for Natalie to close the door after her, the redoubtable Miss Plummer gunned the motor and the car plunged back onto the road.

The speedometer immediately shot up to seventy, and Natalie flinched. Miss Plummer noticed her agitation at once.

"Sorry," she said. "With Doctor out on call, I can't be away too long."

"Oh, yes, the house guests. He told me."

"Did he now?" Miss Plummer took a sharp turn at a crossroads and the tires screeched in protest, but to no avail. Natalie decided to drown apprehension in conversation.

"What sort of a man is my uncle?" she asked.

"Have you never met him?"

"No. My parents moved to Australia when I was quite young. This is my first trip to England. In fact, it's the first time I've left Canberra."

"Folks with you?"

"They were in a motor smashup two months ago," Natalie said. "Didn't the Doctor tell you?"

"I'm afraid not—you see, I haven't been with him very long." Miss Plummer uttered a short bark and the car swerved wildly across the road. "Motor smashup, eh? Some people have no business behind the wheel. That's what Doctor says."

She turned and peered at Natalie. "I take it you've come to stay, then?"

"Yes, of course. He wrote me when he was appointed my guardian. That's why I was wondering what he might be like. It's so hard to tell from letters." The thin-faced woman nodded silently, but Natalie had an urge to confide. "To tell the truth, I'm just a little bit edgy. I mean, I've never met a psychiatrist before."

"Haven't you, now?" Miss Plummer shrugged. "You're quite fortunate. I've seen a few in my time. A bit on the know-it-all side, if you ask me. Though I must say, Dr. Bracegirdle is one of the best. Permissive, you know."

"I understand he has quite a practice."

"There's no lack of patients for *that* sort of thing," Miss Plummer observed. "Particularly amongst the well-to-do. I'd say your uncle has done himself handsomely. The house and all—but you'll see." Once again the wagon whirled into a sickening swerve and sped forward between the imposing gates of a huge driveway which led towards an enormous house set amidst a grove of trees in the distance. Through the shuttered windows Natalie caught sight of a faint beam of light—just enough to help reveal the ornate facade of her uncle's home.

"Oh, dear," she muttered, half to herself.

"What is it?"

"The guests—and it's Saturday night. And here I am, all mussed from travel."

"Don't give it another thought," Miss Plummer assured her. "There's no formality here. That's what the Doctor told me when I came. It's a home away from home."

Miss Plummer barked and braked simultaneously, and the station wagon came to an abrupt stop just behind an imposing black limousine.

"Out with you now!" With brisk efficiency, Miss Plummer lifted the bag from the rear seat and carried it up the steps, beckoning Natalie forward with a nod over her shoulder. She halted at the door and fumbled for a key.

"No sense knocking," she said. "They'd never hear me." As the door swung open her observation was amply confirmed. The background noise which Natalie had noted over the telephone now formed a formidable foreground. She stood there, hesitant, as Miss Plummer swept forward across the threshold.

"Come along, come along!"

Obediently, Natalie entered, and as Miss Plummer shut the door behind her, blinked with eyes unaccustomed to the brightness of the interior.

She found herself standing in a long, somewhat bare hallway. Directly ahead of her was a large staircase; at an angle between the railing and the wall was a desk and chair. To her left, a dark, panelled door—evidently leading to Dr. Bracegirdle's private office, for a small brass plate was affixed to it, bearing his name. To her right was a huge open parlor, its windows heavily curtained and shuttered against the night. It was from here that the sounds of sociability echoed.

Natalie started down the hall toward the stairs. As she did so, she caught a glimpse of the parlor. Fully a dozen guests eddied about a large table, talking and gesturing with the animation of close acquaintance—with one another, and with the contents of the lavish array of bottles gracing the tabletop. A sudden whoop of laughter indicated that at least one guest had abused the Doctor's hospitality.

Natalie passed the entry hastily, so as not to be observed, then glanced behind her to make sure that Miss Plummer was following with her bag. Miss Plummer was indeed following, but her hands were empty. And as Natalie reached the stairs, Miss Plummer shook her head.

"You didn't mean to go up now, did you?" she murmured. "Come in and introduce yourself."

"I thought I might freshen up a bit first."

"Let me go on ahead and get your room in order. Doctor didn't give me notice, you know."

"Really, it's not necessary. I could do with a wash—"

"Doctor should be back any moment now. Do wait for him." Miss Plummer grasped Natalie's arm and with the same speed and expedition she had bestowed on driving, now steered the girl forward into the lighted room.

"Here's Doctor's niece," she announced. "Miss Natalie Rivers, from Australia."

Several heads turned in Natalie's direction, though Miss Plummer's voice had scarcely penetrated the general conversational din. A short, jolly-looking fat man bobbed towards Natalie, waving a half-empty glass.

"All the way from Australia, eh?" He extended his goblet. "You must be thirsty. Here, take this. I'll get another." And before Natalie could reply, he turned and plunged back into the group around the table.

"Major Hamilton," Miss Plummer whispered. "A dear soul, really. Though I'm afraid he's just a wee bit squiffy."

As Miss Plummer moved away, Natalie glanced uncertainly at the glass in her hand. She was not quite sure where to dispose of it.

"Allow me." A tall, gray-haired and quite distinguished-looking man with a black moustache moved forward and took the stemware from between her fingers.

"Thank you."

"Not at all. I'm afraid you'll have to excuse the Major. The party spirit, you know." He nodded, indicating a woman in extreme *décolletage* chattering animatedly to a group of three laughing men. "But since it's by way of being a farewell celebration—"

"Ah, there you are!" The short man whom Miss Plummer had identified as Major Hamilton bounced back into orbit around Natalie, a fresh drink in his hand and a fresh smile on his ruddy face. "I'm back again," he announced. "Just like a boomerang, eh?"

He laughed explosively, then paused. "I say, you *do*

have boomerangs in Australia? Saw quite a bit of you Aussies at Gallipoli. Of course that was some time ago, before *your* time, I daresay—"

"Please, Major." The tall man smiled at Natalie. There was something reassuring about his presence, and something oddly familiar, too. Natalie wondered where she might have seen him before. She watched while he moved over to the Major and removed the drink from his hand.

"Now see here—" the Major spluttered.

"You've had enough, old boy. And it's almost time for you to go."

"One for the road—" The Major glanced around, his hands waving in appeal. "Everyone *else* is drinking!" He made a lunge for his glass, but the tall man evaded him. Smiling at Natalie over his shoulder, he drew the Major to one side and began to mutter to him earnestly in low tones. The Major nodded exaggeratedly, drunkenly.

Natalie looked around the room. Nobody was paying the least attention to her except one elderly woman who sat quite alone on a stool before the piano. She regarded Natalie with a fixed stare that made her feel like an intruder on a gala scene. Natalie turned away hastily and again caught sight of the woman in *décolletage*. She suddenly remembered her own desire to change her clothing and peered at the doorway, seeking Miss Plummer. But Miss Plummer was nowhere to be seen.

Walking back into the hall, she peered up the staircase.

"Miss Plummer!" she called.

There was no response.

Then, from out of the corner of her eye, she noted that the door of the room across the hallway was ajar. In fact, it was opening now, quite rapidly, and as Natalie stared, Miss Plummer came backing out of the room, carrying a pair of scissors in her hand. Before Natalie could call out again and attract her attention, Miss Plummer had scurried off in the other direction.

The people here, Natalie told herself, certainly seemed odd. But wasn't that always the case with people at parties? She crossed before the stairs, meaning to follow Miss

Plummer, but found herself halting before the open doorway.

She gazed in curiously at what was obviously her uncle's consultation room. It was a cosy, book-lined study with heavy, leather-covered furniture grouped before the shelves. The psychiatric couch rested in one corner near the wall and near it was a large mahogany desk. The top of the desk was quite bare, save for a cradle telephone, and a thin brown loop snaking out from it.

Something about the loop disturbed Natalie and before she was conscious of her movement she was inside the room, looking down at the desk-top and the brown cord from the phone.

And then she realized what had bothered her, the end of the cord had been neatly severed from its connection in the wall.

"Miss Plummer!" Natalie murmured, remembering the pair of scissors she'd seen her holding. *But why would she have cut the phone cord?*

Natalie turned just in time to observe the tall, distinguished-looking man enter the doorway behind her.

"The phone won't be needed," he said, as if he'd read her thoughts. "After all, I *did* tell you it was a farewell celebration." And he gave a little chuckle.

Again Natalie sensed something strangely familiar about him, and this time it came to her. She'd heard the same chuckle over the phone, when she'd called from the station.

"You must be playing a joke!" she exclaimed. "You're Dr. Bracegirdle, aren't you?"

"No, my dear." He shook his head as he moved past her across the room. "It's just that no one expected you. We were about to leave when your call came. So we had to say *some*thing."

There was a moment of silence. Then, "Where *is* my uncle?" Natalie asked, at last.

"Over here."

Natalie found herself standing beside the tall man, gazing

down at what lay in a space between the couch and the wall. An instant was all she could bear.

"Messy," the tall man nodded. "Of course it was all so sudden, the opportunity, I mean. And then they *would* get into the liquor—"

His voice echoed hollowly in the room and Natalie realized the sounds of the party had died away. She glanced up to see them all standing there in the doorway, watching.

Then their ranks parted and Miss Plummer came quickly into the room, wearing an incongruous fur wrap over the rumpled, ill-fitting uniform.

"Oh my!" she gasped. "So you found him!"

Natalie nodded and took a step forward. "You've got to do something," she said. "Please!"

"Of course, you didn't see the others," Miss Plummer said, "since they're upstairs. The Doctor's staff. Gruesome sight."

The men and women had crowded into the room behind Miss Plummer, staring silently.

Natalie turned to them in appeal. "Why, it's the work of a madman!" she cried. "He belongs in an asylum!"

"My dear child," murmured Miss Plummer, as she quickly closed and locked the door and the silent starers moved forward. "This *is* an asylum . . ."

HIGH TIDE

by Richard Hardwick

GRADUALLY the outward flow slowed, until imperceptibly all movement of the water had ceased. Almost at once the tide would start to move in again from the sea in its endless cycle, rising in the sound, then in the river, and finally in the creek that cut in against the low bluff before Ray Garvin's nearly completed house.

Across the creek from the unpainted dock a brisk northeast wind made waves in the tall marsh grass that stretched like a bright green meadow all the way to the river, a quarter of a mile away.

His arms resting on the rail, Lloyd Reed stood near the end of the dock and looked down at the man in the skiff.

"What kind of shape is it in, Ray?"

Ray Garvin poled the heavy skiff to shore and climbed out onto the mucky creekbank, tossing the line up to Reed.

"It'll take some work if this thing's going to hold the monorail."

He took a jackknife from his pocket, unclasped it, and dug the long blade at a piling, testing the soundness of the wood.

"How old would you say this dock is, Lloyd? Ten, twenty years?"

"I don't know if it's the same one, but there was a dock here when I was a kid. I remember coming out here with my old man, and that's been better than twenty-five years ago," Reed said.

Garvin folded the knife and dropped it back into the pocket. "It would have been a good thing if it had burned along with the old house." He moved beneath the dock and took hold of a cross brace. "I suppose I ought to take it down and start from scratch." He shook the timber, holding it with both hands and putting his weight into it.

"*Hey!*" Reed yelled. "Don't *shake* it down!"

Garvin thought of the three steel beams piled on the dock above him, and he made a mental note to have the workmen take them off Monday and stack them ashore on the bluff. Might as well be on the safe side.

He shook the brace a final time and turned it loose.

"I'd take it easy down there, Ray," Reed said. "These beams aren't stacked too well—"

His words were cut off suddenly by an abrupt sound, like the crack of a heavy rifle. It came from directly above Garvin, sending a shower of splinters and powdery rotted wood after it.

Garvin's reaction was instinctive, even before Reed's shouted, unintelligible warning. The thought was instantaneous, to get out from under the dock. He threw himself toward the side, but his canvas shoes slipped on the muck and he sprawled forward. Above him came the heavy clang of metal striking metal.

The beams are coming down! Get out of here! His mind froze on the thought as he scrambled on all fours over the slick surface, like a man running in a dream, straining every muscle, yet getting nowhere. He reached the piling, pulled himself past it. *I've made it . . . Another couple of feet—*

Something pushed down suddenly against his right ankle, sending a shock of pain up his leg. It held him fast, and he could hear himself screaming out against the pain. Then there was silence for a moment, and something dropped with a belated splash into the edge of the creek, like the period at the end of a paragraph.

Garvin lay with his face down against the wet muck, his fists clenched, his eyes tightly shut, trying to overcome the pain in the ankle. *The leg is broken. The damned beams fell through, and now my leg is broken . . .*

"Ray! Ray!"

He raised his head and looked toward the bluff. Reed

was hobbling down clumsily, slipping and sliding down the creek bank toward him.

"Ray! Are you all right!"

"I guess I didn't know my own strength," he said, trying to summon a smile. "A regular Samson."

Reed stopped beside him and looked down at the leg. "Can you—can you get your leg out?"

"I don't know." He raised the upper part of his body higher, propping himself on his elbows and turning his head so that he could see the ankle. One of the steel I-beams lay across the ankle, pressing it down into the muck. "I'll try . . ." Garvin pulled, but again the pain seared up his leg. He groaned and let the leg go limp.

"The ankle's broken, I'm sure of that."

"I guess you were lucky," Reed said. "Two of the beams missed you."

"Sure, I was real lucky. Now get this thing off me."

Reed looked at him blankly. "Get it *off* you? That's a ten-inch beam, Ray. It must weigh four hundred pounds or more. You're damn lucky it didn't cut your leg clean off, falling that far!"

"Will you stop telling me how lucky I am and *do* something?"

Reed shrugged and scratched his head. He knelt beside Garvin's foot and peered closely at the place where the beam lay across the leg. The end of the beam rested against the dock piling. He scratched his head again. "My gosh, Ray, you know this back of mine. No chance of me trying to lift this off you. It's a strain to lift a can of beer.

Garvin knew Lloyd's back, all right. Everybody knew about the back. It was Lloyd's claim to fame, the way he'd gotten it when he was a gunner aboard a B-17 and had to parachute out of the burning plane over the English channel. It was also Lloyd's only source of steady income, his disability pension.

"I didn't mean to yell at you, Lloyd." He closed his eyes for a moment, trying to think. "Maybe you can dig out beneath the leg and then I can slide out."

"Sure! That ought to work!"

Reed began to dig down beside the ankle with both hands. He touched the leg once and Garvin stiffened.

"Sorry, Ray . . ."

He went on digging at the thick muck. Garvin glanced to his right and saw that the skiff was now afloat where he had beached it only minutes before. "The tide's started in," he said. "I've got to get out of here."

"The tide?" Reed paused and moved back on his haunches. He looked at the creek, an odd expression sifting over his face. "Spring tide, too. With this northeaster it'll hit eleven feet—"

"For heaven's sake, Lloyd, will you shut up and get *busy!*"

He bent quickly to his task again, digging silently around the ankle. After a while he stopped. "Ray . . ." He cleared his throat nervously. "Ray, there's something under your leg, an old timber or broken piling or something. That beam's got you pinned down against it."

Through the steady throb of pain, Garvin experienced, for the first time, a sudden small spurt of fear. He raised himself on his elbows, then pushed up with his hands until he was standing erect on his knees. The movement had brought with it excruciating pain, but now at least he was that much higher above the level of the water only a few inches to his right.

"What . . . what'll we do?" Lloyd said.

If we can't go down, then we've got to come up. "We have to raise the I-beam somehow." He cast his gaze toward the bluff, his mind racing, trying to pick up some glimmer of an idea. Beyond the bluff he saw the top of Lloyd's car. There was power. Now, some way to transmit the power where it was needed . . .

He looked up at the broken dock. The decking was gone where the beams had come through, but the side timber atop the piling seemed intact, and the cross beam that rested on it.

"Lloyd, run a rope over that beam. Tie one end to your car and the other we can slip beneath the I-beam. All we need to do is to get it up a few inches—"

"Where's any rope?"

"Rope?" Garvin looked around quickly. He reached out to his right and snagged the painter of the skiff. "Here's some rope. It's not too old—"

Reed interrupted again. "That's not more than twenty or thirty feet long, Ray. We'll need at least a hundred to get to the car."

Garvin stared at the rope in his hand. Lloyd was right about it. It was not nearly long enough. He flung it away from him. "What about the car? Haven't you got any in the car?"

Reed shrugged and shook his head.

There was a new coil of half-inch manila in the trunk of Garvin's car, but they hadn't come in his car. No rope on the dock or around the new house. The eighteen-foot outboard had a good long nylon anchor line aboard, but it was on its trailer in the garage in town.

He felt something against his knees and looked down. The creek was rising rapidly. An eleven-foot tide, Reed had said. Eleven feet in six and a half hours. Better than a foot and a half an hour. What is the distance from a man's knees to his nose? Four feet? That meant something like two and a half hours and if he wasn't out from under the steel beam . . .

"Lloyd . . ."

"You thought of something?"

Garvin turned his head and looked into Reed's eyes. "You've got to go for help. A couple of able-bodied men could lift the end of this thing high enough for me to slip my foot out."

Reed got to his feet, nodding. "I guess you're right. Let's see, it's only five or six miles into town. Maybe I can find Tom Forman. He's got a back like an ape. And Julius—"

"Lloyd," Garvin said slowly, rubbing one hand across his forehead. "Lloyd, this ankle hurts like merry hell. The tide is coming in. Will you please *go? Go!*"

"Yeah. Sure." He moved away, starting up the sloping creekbank. Halfway to the bluff he looked around. "I was going to tell you to wait here for me, but that wouldn't have been so funny, would it?" He slapped his shirt pocket quickly. "Hey! You got any cigarettes? Want me to leave mine with you?"

Garvin reached inside the open jacket. The cigarettes were there in the pocket of his shirt, but when he had fallen forward they had been ruined by the muck. "I would like a cigarette before you go."

Reed came back down, gave Garvin the pack and his matches. "I'll be back, Ray. You just . . . well, you just take it easy, huh?"

"I'll be all right."

Reed made his way toward the bluff again, but Garvin called after him. "Lloyd, *you* take it easy. Nobody but you knows I'm stuck here . . ." He stopped, feeling a sudden regret for having said it.

"Check." Reed looked at him for a moment, turned and scrambled up the bluff and disappeared.

The car door slammed, the motor roared to life, and the car pulled away. The sound of it faded very quickly.

For a time silence seemed to descend on him, and then, gradually, as if his senses had been honed razor-sharp, Garvin became aware of the sound of the wind. The lonely restlessness as it moved through the live oaks along the bluff, the sibilant, whispering sound it made in the marsh grass across the creek. A feeling of isolation, of utter solitude and helplessness crept like a heavy hand over his heart.

He thought of Lloyd Reed. Given his choice of a man with whom to entrust his life, it occurred to him that Lloyd would have been far down the list. Yet, why did he feel this way? They had grown up together, known each other since earliest memory. Still, his final admonition had instantly brought on an odd sensation, a feeling of distrust. Friendship should be synonymous with trust.

Perhaps that was it. This relation with Lloyd Reed, was it really friendship, or merely an acquaintance of long standing?

He looked down. The water had already risen to his knees. The injured foot was completely covered. He lifted his arm and looked at his watch for the first time. The hands stood at eleven-fifteen. Mary would be at church now with her sister, Eleanor. Lloyd had been gone ten or fifteen minutes and that meant at least another twenty before he got back.

Somewhere across the creek a marsh hen cackled, and another responded downstream toward the river. It would be a good tide for hunting. The water would cover the marsh.

But the familiar sounds of the birds served only to increase this feeling of being utterly alone. Even the mounting pain in the ankle, throbbing with each beat of his pulse, did not take his thoughts off . . . off what?

It was simply a matter of time. In a few minutes Lloyd would be back with help and they would take him to the hospital to have the ankle attended to. He'd have to wear a cast for a while, walk with crutches . . .

He lifted the watch again. The minute hand was straight down. Eleven-thirty. Garvin lowered his arm, realizing as he did so that the fingers now touched the water. He cocked his head, listening for some sound above the wind and water.

Nothing.

He turned his face up to the sky. Beneath the high gray overcast of the northeaster a lone gull angled off on the wind, gliding toward some roost to wait out the storm, or until hunger forced him aloft again.

Garvin shifted his weight, trying to bring his good leg up, but stopping as the movement brought a new burst of pain. It couldn't be much longer now. Lloyd had been gone at least half an hour.

He pulled the front of the muck-spattered jacket together and buttoned it against the chill that crept up his body from the water. This was typical of Lloyd, never on time, completely undependable. Lloyd had never married, and seldom held a job over six months. He lived carelessly, worked sloppily, didn't seem to have a care or ambition beyond the present moment.

Damn it! Can't he realize what I'm going through!

Garvin's face grew thoughtful. Was Lloyd really the way he seemed? Or was it a front that had been developed over the years? He recalled an incident that had taken place only a few weeks ago. Lloyd was in the office and Mary had come in. They had just bought this property and were involved in all the plans for the new house.

Garvin remembered how Lloyd sat quietly on the corner of the desk, listening to Mary's excited chatter about materials and colors and landscaping, and Ray's plans for the monorail for the boat.

Lloyd had watched Mary when she left, and after a moment turned around to face Garvin with a strange, lonely look. "You're lucky, Ray. I wonder if you really know how damn lucky you are—a good wife, good business, new house, dough in the bank." He lowered his eyes, picked up a pencil and slowly tapped it on the desktop. "Time gets away from you." When he looked up again there had been something like bitterness in his voice. "I envy you, boy."

But the mood had been ephemeral, and immediately he fell back into character.

"Come on, close the joint up! Everything's perfect for trout this afternoon! They ought to practically jump into the boat!"

Had it been something noted and said on the spur of the moment? Maybe it had been Mary. Lloyd had dated her the last two years they were in high school. Perhaps for a moment he glimpsed that which all men see fleetingly from time to time; what might have been.

Until now, Garvin had thought nothing of it. Again he looked at his watch and saw that Lloyd had been gone forty-five minutes. The creek had risen with surprising rapidity and the water now reached the top of his thighs. What could have happened to him? He could have had a flat, or run out of gas.

There was quite obviously nothing to do but wait, and Garvin tried to occupy his mind with ideas about a new dock.

But by noon, with the water swirling about his hips, he told himself the thing that had crawled slowly up from the depths of his mind. *He is not coming back. Lloyd is going to leave me here to die . . .*

Out in the open it was coldly logical. An opportunity, completely unforeseen and thus completely unplanned, had arisen. With a bit of luck Lloyd could take over Ray Garvin's life, lock, stock, and barrel. He could pick it up where Garvin left off, the way a relay runner takes the baton and moves ahead, taking with him all the advantage that has been built up to that point.

Mary liked him. The fact was, nobody *disliked* Lloyd Reed. But Mary and Lloyd had sort of gone steady in school and it was not at all inconceivable that with Garvin dead the old romance could be slowly rekindled. Mary was not a woman meant to live alone. After a proper interval, with gentle insistence from Lloyd . . .

Garvin suddenly struck the water with his fist. A deadening sense of impotence swept over him. His own survival palled. Somehow he had to leave a warning for Mary, tell her in some way this thing was not wholly an accident.

Yet, could he be wrong? *Had* something happened to Lloyd?

The hands of the watch stood at ten minutes past twelve. The water was at his waist. In less than an hour and a half it wouldn't matter if Lloyd got back with help or not.

He took another cigarette from Lloyd's pack. His hands shook and the pack dropped into the water.

"Damn—"

He watched the pack drift away on the tide, turning in the little swirls made by his own body. He lit the cigarette and threw the rest of the matches after the cigarettes.

Well, this must be it. He took a long, deep drag on the cigarette, watching the wind tear the smoke away as he exhaled. *A last smoke for the condemned man.*

What was Lloyd Reed doing now? Right this minute. Was he somewhere keeping an eye on the time, figuring the rise of the water and waiting? Could he really *do* it?

There were so many things yet to do. Garvin was thirty-six. He had worked hard, made headway, been neither miserly nor wasteful and was within sight of many of his goals. This place, this was one of the big ones.

With all that lay ahead, to be here trapped like an animal, watching the minutes slip past . . .

He paused, the cigarette inches from his lips. *Like an animal?* He looked down quickly at the water swirling about him just below his ribs, and he reached down tentatively, feeling the cold, heavy beam laying across his leg. He straightened again and took the jackknife from his pocket. He looked at the long blade, folded in against the handle. There were animals that would gnaw a leg off if it was caught in a trap. Could a man . . . could a man actually *cut off his own foot* . . .

Quickly he thrust the knife into the pocket of his jacket, repelled by the thought. There was time yet. He looked at the watch. Twenty minutes before one. But Lloyd had been gone more than an hour and a half. He was not coming back.

If I could see him afterwards, just for a moment, I would know. It would be there in his eyes. Perhaps Mary will see it.

The water climbed his chest. In less than an hour it would be above his chin, he would be straining upward for air, pulling against the trapped leg.

He felt for the knife again. It was the only way. The alternative was death.

He turned his eyes toward the shore, following the line of the bluff in the direction of the house. It stood there, out of sight, beneath the twin oaks near the turn of the creek, with a sweeping view of the broad marshlands and the distant blue of the sea. There would be nights, quiet windless nights, when you could hear fish jumping in the creek, and the faint faraway thunder of the surf on the bar at the mouth of the sound.

A man with one leg would be able to hear that, see it. A dead man would hear and see nothing.

Suddenly he froze, cocking his head. Was it imagination, or had that been the sound of an engine? Maybe Lloyd *was* coming back, after all . . .

There it was again! It was a boat, an outboard by the

high sound of it. The sound came on the wind from the river. Only a fool would be fishing in a northeaster, but someone *was* out there.

His impulse was to call out, but the futility was obvious. The boat was upwind, at least a quarter of a mile away. A last wavering sound came on the wind and then it was gone, leaving a deeper void for its having existed at all.

After a while, when he was certain that the boat had gone, he lifted the knife from the water. *Can I do it? Maybe it will be so painful that I will pass out.*

He took the knife in both hands and pulled it open. He let his thumb move along the blade. The blade was sharp. A dull knife was little better than no knife at all.

If I can do it beneath the beam where the bone is broken . . .

There would be blood, quite a lot of it. He thought of the shark he had caught last summer less than a mile from this spot while he had been tarpon fishing. It had been something over eight feet long. Wasn't blood supposed to attract sharks? Maybe they weren't here this time of the year, or maybe the ones here were not man-eaters.

He reached down again and touched the trapped leg. The pain had become a dull throb and the ankle was swollen. The mere contact of his fingertips brought a great stab of pain.

Get on with it! Quit stalling! No one is coming here to help you . . . The tide is not going to wait!

Then he looked around, his eyes went to the dock above him and then to the knife in his hand, and strangely, a slow smile crept over his face. The tide! *The tide!* How could he have overlooked it. The smile broadened and after a moment Garvin began to laugh.

The dark water moved past the dock, swirling and eddying about the pilings, filling the bed of the creek. Gradually, an alien sound emerged above the wind. A car, traveling as fast as the twisting drive would allow, appeared through the trees. Tom Forman sat behind the wheel and beside him, Lloyd Reed, a white bandage wrapped about his head. In the rear of the car were Doc Sanders and Julius Mason.

The car pulled as close to the dock as it could get. The four doors flew open, the men piling out. Reed was the first to reach the dock, and he stopped short, his eyes scanning the creek. There was nothing, only the broken dock and the water.

"We're too late! I knew it!"

"Where was he?" Forman said.

"Down there." He pointed. "See where the planking's smashed, that's where the steel beams went through. It was terrible. Ray was just underneath . . ."

"Hey!" a voice called.

The four men turned toward the sound. Ray Garvin sat below them at the edge of the creekbank, his back propped against the bluff. The jackknife was in his hand and the muck-smeared jacket lying over the lower portion of his legs.

"What took you so long, Lloyd?" he said.

"You're . . . you're *alive* . . . ?" Reed's voice was little more than a hoarse whisper. He stared down at Garvin and his eyes moved to the jacket. "How . . . how did you—"

"I asked you, Lloyd. What took you so long?" Garvin said.

Doc Sanders moved to the edge of the bluff. "He said you were pinned under a steel beam, Ray. Somebody come along and help you out?"

"Nobody helped me out. I want to know what happened to Lloyd."

"I—I got to hurrying, Ray . . . The car went off the road, smacked into a pine tree." He reached up quickly and touched the bandage. "Knocked me out. I was out for I don't know how long . . ."

"I know how long. About three hours. You watch the time pretty closely when you're in the situation I was in. It'd surprise you just how fast the tide comes in when you don't want it to. You do a lot of thinking, you wonder how you're going to feel when the water starts lapping under your nose."

The doctor made his way down the bluff. When he reached Garvin he knelt by his side. "Let me take a look at that leg." He started to lift the jacket.

"Wait a minute, Doc," Garvin said.

"But if it's broken—"

"In a minute," Garvin's eyes were on Lloyd Reed. "You think of all sorts of things. And while I was thinking, I thought of this." He held up the jackknife, the blade open and glinting dully. "I remembered stories of how some animals will chew off a leg that's caught in a trap."

Reed's mouth dropped open. He raised one hand, pointing toward the covered legs. "You mean . . ." His eyes blinked rapidly, he swallowed. "You . . . *you cut your foot off . . .*"

The other men stared. Garvin folded the knife slowly. "I thought about it for a long time. I waited for somebody to come. I prayed. And all the time the water kept coming up. It reached my waist, my ribs, chest. I had to hold my arms up to keep them out of the water."

The doctor reached for the jacket. "You better let me see that, Ray—"

He pushed the doctor's hand aside, and went on. "I figured the bone was pretty well broken, so there'd be no problem with that. I wondered about the pain, and whether I could stay conscious while I was doing it—"

"Oh my God. . . ." Reed murmured.

Garvin smiled, folded the knife and pushed it into his pants pocket. "And then I thought about something else, something so simple that it made me laugh."

"What the devil *was* it?" Mason said.

"The skiff, it was tied up right beside me."

"It's not there now."

"It drifted around the bend a while ago."

"But how did—"

"It was tied up on the dock, but with the jackknife I reached as far up the line as I could and cut it."

The corners of Doc Sanders' eyes crinkled and he nodded. "You tied it to the beam, and when the tide rose, the skiff rose with it."

"And it . . . it lifted the beam off you?" said Forman.

The doctor reached down and picked up the jacket. Both feet were there, the right one bent over at an odd angle. "Get my bag out of the car, Tom," he said. "And one of you drive to a phone and get an ambulance." He looked at Garvin. "I think we'd better take you out of here on a stretcher, Ray."

"Sure, Doc."

The black medical bag was brought down to the doctor. Garvin continued to look at Lloyd Reed. It was there in his eyes, the guilt. There was no disguising it.

The doctor held a syringe in his hand. He wiped a place on Garvin's arm and pushed the needle in. "That'll ease the pain."

Garvin nodded absently. "Lloyd?"

"Ray . . . I . . ." His gaze wavered, his face grew pale.

What good was an accusation? The wound on Reed's head would be real enough, it would have to be, for without it there would be doubt in the minds of the others.

But the two of them knew what had happened.

"Lloyd . . ." *Let him live with it.* "The cigarettes got wet, Lloyd. Got any more?" *Let him live with it. If he can . . .*

THE WORLD'S OLDEST MOTIVE

by Laurence M. Janifer

SITTING IN THE QUIET little bedroom of Flora's East-side apartment, Philip Devize breathed a little sigh and realized, with a small shock of surprise, that he was perfectly happy. A man of forty-three, he told himself judiciously, had no business feeling as free as the air and as young as Pat Boone, but there it was; he felt wonderful. There was no use in denying it.

Of course, Flora herself had something to do with it—marvelous Flora, young and enthusiastic and beautiful. Who would have thought she'd have been so violently attracted to a middle-aged man? Philip hardly thought of himself as aging, bald or pot-bellied, but he had few illusions about his looks. At forty-three, dashing handsomeness was quite out of the picture, after all. Yet Flora had seen something in him, some quality that had caught and held her . . .

But Flora wasn't the answer. He'd spent evenings with Flora before, evenings when his wife thought he was working late or out of town and he'd never felt quite so free, quite so happy.

He smiled quietly to himself. The reason for his cheer was perfectly obvious, after all. It was the murder, of course.

Flora snuggled closer to him on the big red couch. "Penny," she said.

Philip blinked. "Oh, nothing," he said. "Nothing at all. Just thinking how—how happy I am. With you, and everything."

"I'm glad," Flora said throatily. "Tell me, darling. Do I make you very happy?"

"Of course you do," Philip said, rather theatrically, and gathered her in his arms. Several seconds passed.

"That's all I want," Flora said with a sigh. "To make you very happy."

Philip kissed her again. "Nothing else?"

"But, darling," Flora said. "I love you. What else could I want?"

Philip thought of his wife and grimaced. "Attention," he said. "Attention all the time, every fool minute. Clothes. Furs. Jewels. Why, Flora, do you only want to make me happy?"

"Because I love you," Flora said throatily.

"And I—I love you," Philip said. He folded her in his arms, feeling perfectly content, and thinking, with a tiny part of his mind, about the murder.

Philip had read too many detective stories to think that he could get away with killing his wife. In such cases, as he was well aware, it is the husband who is the first and usually the only suspect. And, given that initial suspicion, a well-equipped modern police force like the ones he'd read about would inevitably find evidence to back it up. Philip, though his wish to slough off his wife—like an old, outgrown and unpleasant skin—was strong, had no concomitant desire to go to jail or to the electric chair for the deed.

And then—it was wonderfully coincidental when he thought of it—he'd met Flora, and Schustak, both at almost the same time.

Flora had come first. It had been in a bar, one not too far from his own apartment in the East 70's. She had come in and seen him there, and suddenly they were talking together. It had all seemed so natural . . . and then, there had been more meetings, and at last he had gone to Flora's apartment, and that had really been the start.

He wondered just how far he would have allowed himself to go with Flora, if he had not meet Schustak in the meantime. He would probably have done all the same things, he reflected; after all, by the time he did meet Schustak, Flora knew all there was to know about him, from his boyhood right on up to the marriage he'd have given anything to be rid of.

Naturally, she'd asked him about a possible divorce. But a divorce was out of the question, he knew; he told her so. His wife would never have agreed to such a thing; all her upbringing was against it, and besides—he told Flora, with a wry smile—she wasn't going to let go of a gold mine.

He had money; his family had been well-to-do for several generations, and Philip's father had increased their holdings until "fortune" was the only really right word. Perhaps Philip's wife had married him for money originally; he wouldn't have put it past her, he said. At any rate, divorce was impossible.

He never mentioned murder, of course. Not to Flora. Discussing detective stories was as far as he ever went in that line; Flora and murder just didn't go together. It wasn't exactly that she was innocent, but Philip didn't want to talk about anything unpleasant when he was with her. He wanted things to be perfect, as far as Flora was concerned.

And they were, or at least Flora said so. She kept her own apartment, refused gifts from him—lived her own life. "Only it's your life now, darling," she had said. "It belongs to you—because I belong to you."

The next morning, Schustak had come to his office.

"He says it's about a Miss Flora Arnold," Philip's secretary told him.

Philip went white, but managed to control himself. "Show him in," he said, and when Schustak walked in, thin, dapper, completely at ease with his small, precise movements, Philip said only: "Close the door."

Schustak said: "Of course," and did so. He sat down opposite Philip, across the desk.

Philip took a deep breath. "You mentioned Flora Arnold to my secretary," he said.

Schustak nodded, moving his head perhaps three-quarters of an inch. "Exactly," he said, and took out a gold cigarette case. He extracted a cigarette, lit it, put the case back and went on: "I am sorry to cause you any discomfort. But it was the only sure way of being admitted to your private office without disclosing my real motives."

"I don't want Flora's name—Miss Arnold's name—used in—" Philip got that far, and stopped. "Your real motives?" he said, in an entirely different voice. "Blackmail, I suppose." He shook his head. "You're out of luck, Mr. Schuman, or whatever your name is. I won't pay a cent."

"Schustak," Schustak said. "And I have no wish to blackmail you. On the contrary. I am here to do you a service."

Philip nodded. "Sure you are," he said bitterly. "You know about Flora, so you figure I want it kept quiet. Well —"

"Will you dismiss Miss Arnold from your mind?" Schustak said quietly. "I merely used her name to see you. I do not know the woman; I have never met her; I have no wish to meet her. My business has little, if any, connection with her. I am here to serve you."

Philip closed his eyes for a second. When he opened them, he still felt a little dizzy. "You don't know her," he said. "Then how do you know her name?"

"Because," Mr. Schustak said carefully, "I know you." He tapped his cigarette into Philip's desk ashtray, and went on: "Not in the personal sense, of course. But I know of your troubles with your—ah—wife. I know of your wish for a solution." He smiled, very slightly. "I am here to offer that solution," he said.

"My wife," Philip said tightly, "is my own business. So is Fl—— Miss Arnold. And I don't see what right you have to come barging in here and—"

"Right?" Schustak said. "But you invited me in." He raised a hand, forestalling Philip for a second. "And I must somehow make you believe me, Mr. Devize; I am interested only in helping you. I have a solution for your—ah—difficulty."

Philip grimaced. In spite of himself, he was beginning to

believe the man. "There isn't any solution," he said.

"There is one," Schustak said carefully.

Philip blinked. The silence seemed to last forever.

"Mr. Devize," Schustak said at last. "You read detective fiction."

"How do you know?" Philip asked.

Schustak shrugged. "I also know about Miss Arnold," he pointed out, "and about your wife. Our organization is especially proud of its research branch."

"Organization?" Philip said.

Schustak nodded. He pressed out his cigarette, neatly. "Let me continue," he said quietly. "You read detective fiction. You have often, perhaps, seen references to some large combine which, for a fee, would—ah—eliminate a designated person."

"Murder, Inc.," Philip said.

Schustak frowned. "By no means as crude as that," he said. "Let us say, simply, that we have a method—a quite undetectable method—of elimination. That method is at your disposal—for a fee."

"It's ridiculous," Philip said.

"Is it?" Schustak said. "And you have read about it so often? It is, in fact, a very old idea. Does it surprise you that it has been translated into reality?"

"But—"

"I understand," Schustak said. "You are—hesitant. Allow me to leave my card; you may call me, of course, any business day. Our offices are open from 9:30 until 5." He took a wallet from his breast pocket, extracted a small, white card and put it on Philip's desk. He rose and went to the door.

"Wait a minute," Philip said suddenly.

Schustak turned slowly. "Yes?" he said.

"You mean—" Philip blinked. "You mean, for a fee, you'll undertake to—to murder my wife for me?"

"I?" Schustak said. "No, Mr. Devize. Naturally not. I am only a salesman. In this age of specialization, Mr. Devize, we have found it wise to hire—specialists."

"But I'll be suspected," Philip said. "They'll find out—

they'll trace things back and find out I hired you, and then —"

" 'They' will do no such thing," Schustak said. " 'They' will never realize that your wife was—ah—murdered. Our techniques are quite satisfactory."

"But—"

"Please call me," Schustak said smoothly, "when you're ready to discuss matters more fully." The door opened, then closed.

Philip stared around at the empty room.

"Hoax," he said to himself—but, of course, he couldn't believe that. Schustak's proposition sounded more and more outrageous as the hours and days passed—but, of course, he couldn't pay any attention to that.

He had hope. He talked everything over with Flora—cautiously, never giving her a hint of the real situation, telling it all to her as if it had happened to a "Friend." He felt proud of himself when he was through; she obviously didn't suspect he was telling her of a real situation, one which concerned him, directly.

Her advice was just what he hoped it would be. "After all, this friend of yours couldn't lose anything by calling up and asking more questions, could he? I mean, what harm could it do? And he could always stop things."

It was exactly what he was thinking himself. The next morning—after some preliminary hesitation, frightening and unexpected—he called the number of Schustak's little white card, and made an appointment.

The office building was an old one, a little run-down. Philip took the elevator to the tenth floor, as Schustak had directed, and found Room 1012 quickly. There was no other lettering on the ground-glass door, and when he opened it, there was nothing inside but a single desk, and Mr. Schustak behind it.

"Our offices are, necessarily, modest," Mr. Schustak said, smiling. "We maintain more elaborate facilities—ah—out of town. Won't you be seated?"

There was a chair next to the desk. Wordlessly, Philip sat down.

"You understand, of course," Schustak said, "that we hardly want to draw attention to ourselves."

"Of course," Philip said absently. He'd read enough to know that. What did the man take him for? "I wanted to talk about this—this method of yours."

"Ah," Schustak said. He closed his eyes. "I'm afraid I can tell you very little about the actual method; it must remain our secret. You understand."

"But—"

"Safety is guaranteed," Schustak said. "After all, were you to be—bothered in any way, we would also be exposed. Please realize that it is to our interest, as well as yours, to see that everything goes off smoothly."

"Of course," Philip said. "I'm—sorry. But it still seems to me that—"

"That you ought to know something?" Schustak said. "Quite rightly." He uttered a single name.

"You mean you—"

Schustak nodded, making it a full inch this time.

"But that was—a natural death," Philip said. "A heart attack."

Schustak nodded. "That was the coroner's report," he said. "You see, our method is really novel, and quite undetectable."

Philip drew a long breath. It seemed to take a long time for him to say: "You mentioned a fee, last time."

Schustak frowned down at his desk for a second. At last he looked up. "Shall we say—ten thousand dollars?"

"Ten. Ten thousand—ridiculous!" Philip said. "I haven't got—"

"Mr. Devize." The voice was suddenly cold. "Do you mistrust our research department? We know—we *know* how much money you have, how much is available. Ten thousand is rather modest.

Philip shook his head. "I won't pay out ten thousand dollars in advance—"

"Of course not," Schustak said. "But five thousand now,

another five thousand upon—ah—satisfactory completion . . ."

"It's too much," Philip said emphatically.

Schustak looked back at the desk. "I'm sorry," he said. "Please don't—ah—slam the door when you leave."

"But—"

"We do not bargain," Schustak said coldly.

It hung in the balance for a full minute.

Then Philip said: "Do you want a check?"

Schustak almost smiled. "Cash," he said. "Bring it here, this afternoon."

His voice was friendly again.

And now—now there was nothing to do but wait. Settled on the red couch with Flora in his arms, Philip smiled slowly. By the time he got home, his wife would be—eliminated. He would be free.

He thought about marriage again—and Flora. A slight frown crossed his face. It might not do to get tied up again, so soon after the—death. Besides, Flora wasn't the only woman who'd be happy to be seen with him, not any more. Not now, when he was free, rich . . .

She moved in his arms. "Darling," she said huskily, "don't you really think that you ought to be going?"

Philip hesitated, then nodded. "I suppose so," he said. "But I'll be back—tomorrow. And maybe I won't have to leave, ever again."

All the way home, he drove without paying attention to the road. He had to be properly grief-stricken, he knew. That didn't promise to be too tough; the only important thing was acting surprised and shocked—and that, he told himself, would be easy.

And then, afterward . . . He smiled and let himself drift into reverie. Freedom—complete, absolute freedom. No more nagging, no more, "Why don't you ever pay attention to me?", no more—well, he thought, no more Mrs. Philip Devize.

He had definitely decided against getting married again

when he reached home. Whistling, he opened the apartment door. Where would she be? he wondered. In the living room, or the kitchen, or in the bedroom? He let the door slam behind him and started forward. He reached out to turn on a light.

"Philip!'"

It was her voice.

She was alive.

And—he discovered rapidly—there had not even been an attempt on her life. She was exactly the same.

Schustak sighed. "By now," he said to the girl next to him, "it's over. He's home, and he knows. It's all over."

"But couldn't he—well, go to the police?" she said.

Schustak shook his head. "With what?" he said. "He hired somebody to kill his wife—and they didn't come through? No, we're safe. Of course, if she'd slipped in the bathtub or something, we could have claimed the credit and collected the other five thousand—but there's no sense in being greedy. And the office is closed—unavoidable overhead, I suppose, but it hurt to pay that first month's rent. We're gone and he'll never find us."

"I think you're wonderful," she said.

"Wonderful?" Schustak said. "For this? Everything was easy—getting the information about him, making the pitch, stringing him, collecting. And getting out. Even the idea isn't a new one—just an adaptation of an old idea, for the especial benefit of a man who reads detective stories. A very old idea."

"Well—I still think you're wonderful," she said, and snuggled close to him.

"Why, Flora!" Schustak said, without any real surprise, and embraced her.

A VERY CAUTIOUS BOY

by Gilbert Ralston

ROSETTI'S RESTAURANT is tucked away in a remodeled brownstone on New York's 46th Street, close enough to Park Avenue to be considered a good address. Once, in the days of the Charleston and the blind pig, it was one of the town's plushier speakeasies. Now it has become one of the string of expensive character restaurants which dot the East Side.

Lee Costa took a moment to remember it as it was in the old days when Fat Joe Waxman owned it, keeping a fatherly eye out for the welfare of the young tenement boys who ran his less dubious errands, with particular solicitude for developing skills of the brightest of these, one of whom was Costa.

His faith was not misplaced. Lee Costa had turned out well. Fat Joe would have been proud of him on this August night as he stood, a compact ruggedly powerful man, amusing himself with nostalgic thoughts, quietly watching a group of opulent-looking customers enter the refurbished establishment.

Costa took another moment to look it over after he made his way past the door. The layout of the place was as he remembered it: a long bar running the length of one wall opposite a row of booths, a dining area, a checkroom at his right.

He stood for a moment in the entranceway near the reservation desk, pausing while a headwaiter made his way out of the gloom.

"I'm looking for Joe Rosetti," Costa said.

"Who shall I say is calling?"

"Tell him the insurance man is here."

"No name?"

"Just tell him. He'll know."

"You may wait in the bar, if you wish."

Costa crossed to the checkroom to leave his coat. As he turned to go toward the bar, he found his way blocked by the hulking form of one of the waiters. "C'mon," he said. "I'll take you up." He jerked a thumb at an ancient elevator in the corner of the room.

The Rosetti apartment was the only one on the fourth floor, the lock on the door opening with a muted buzz after the guide had pressed the doorbell. They entered a living room which spread across a large part of the side of the building, furnished simply and well, a group of heavy antiques giving it a comfortable feeling of old-fashioned luxury.

A rotund little man stood in the doorway of the room, examining Costa with a quizzical eye. "I'm Joe Rosetti," he said, his accent betraying his Italian parentage. He made no move to take Costa's hand, simply stood and looked at him, his head cocked a little to one side, a tiny frown of concentration on his forehead.

"You're smaller than I thought you'd be," he said. "Come in. Sit. You too, Ziggy." He held the door of the interior room open as Costa and his guide passed through. "Meet Lee Costa, Mamma," he said. Across the room a tiny, dark woman raised her head, holding Costa's eyes with her own, searching his face. She sighed, the sound making a little explosive punctuation in the still room. "This is him?" she said.

Rosetti nodded his head.

She stared at Costa as she gathered up her knitting. "Take care of your business, Papa. After, we will eat." She left the room.

Ziggy stood up, looking down at Costa. "This guy bringing you some trouble?" he asked Rosetti.

Rosetti shook his head.

Costa's cold blue eyes were suddenly alert. "If I was bringing trouble, what would you do?"

"Throw you away somewhere," the big man said, taking a step toward him.

Costa turned to Rosetti. "Better chain up your ape." He turned a bland face to the standing man. "Back off, fat boy," he said calmly.

The man started for him, hands reaching for his lapels. As he bent over, Costa's foot shot out, catching him squarely in the midriff. He doubled over with an agonized gasp. Costa went to him, flipping him to the floor with a crash. "Sorry, Mr. Rosetti," Costa said. "He asked for it."

Rosetti leaned across the desk to look at the prone man writhing on the floor. "So fast," he said. "Like a snake."

"You're good at your job, Mr. Rosetti. I'm good at mine."

"He'll kill you," Rosetti said.

Costa shook his head. "No, he won't, Mr. Rosetti. He'll go downstairs and take care of the drunks. Won't you, Ziggy?"

On the floor, the man gasped for breath, turning his head like a wounded turtle. His eyes went to Costa's smiling face.

"Next time," Costa said, "I won't treat you so gently. Remember that."

With an inarticulate grunt, the man staggered to his feet and out of the room.

"Why was Ziggy here, Mr. Rosetti?" Costa asked.

"I was afraid."

"Of me? You don't have to be. I'm a professional. I do what I'm paid for, nothing more."

Rosetti settled back in his chair nervously.

"Go ahead, tell me about it," Costa said. "Our mutual friend said you had a problem."

"I have a problem. That's why I sent for you."

"Tell me the name of the problem, Mr. Rosetti."

"His name is Baxter. Roy Baxter."

"No other way to handle it?"

"I could pay."

"That doesn't usually work with a blackmailer," Costa said.

"You know about it?"

"Only what our friend told me. He said that someone was trying to shake you down.."

Rosetti hesitated.

"Go ahead, Mr. Rosetti. You can trust me."

Rosetti looked away, his face working. "It was a long time ago. I killed a man. Baxter found out about it. He wants money. I know him. He won't stop. He'll never stop, if I did pay. So I called our friend. I did him a favor once. A big one. Now he pays back. With you."

"Have you told your wife?"

"She knows. But she don't talk."

"Anybody else know about me?"

"No. Just me, Mamma and our friend." Rosetti reached into the drawer of his desk. "Here's the addresses for Baxter. His house. His business. A picture."

Costa glanced at the addresses. "What's his business?"

"He's a lawyer. Or says he is. I don't know how he makes his money. He's supposed to have some."

"Why does he want yours, then?"

"I don't know. Maybe he's got expenses."

"Expenses. I have them, too," Costa said.

"I know. I can pay."

"Our friend said to give you the wholesale rate." Costa smiled at him again. "Could you afford five thousand?"

"Yes. What Baxter wants makes that sound like a bargain."

"How much time did he give you?"

"He said he would give me two weeks to raise twenty-five thousand dollars. Then he goes to the police."

Costa stood, carefully tucking the papers into his pocket. "I'll look the situation over. Let you know."

Rosetti looked at him, his hands working. "Please," he said.

"I'm a very cautious boy, Mr. Rosetti. I'll check it out. Let you know." Costa let his eyes wander to the mounted tarpon over the mantel. "You're jumpy," he said. "Why don't you go fishing for a few days?"

Rosetti made a little wry grimace. "Me?" he said. "Every weekend I fish. All summer. Mama and I. Every weekend. We have a little boat. We live quiet. Run the restaurant. Fish. All of a sudden, I get a call from that Baxter. I don't fish. I don't run the restaurant. Just worry."

"I'll do what I can, Mr. Rosetti. Maybe you'll be fishing again soon."

Costa left the room, nodding pleasantly to Mama Rosetti as he passed her in the living room. She looked up, her sad little face following him as he started for the door. "You have your dinner?" she asked.

"Not yet."

"Come downstairs. We'll eat." She crossed to the other door. "Coming, Papa?"

He appeared in the doorway. "Go eat," he said. "While I sleep."

"Cover up good. Papa," she said.

They sat in one of the booths in the restaurant, the little woman saying only a few words while they ate. Finally, after the coffee was served, she looked up at him.

"It is a sad thing," she said. "Papa is so afraid."

"Are you?" Costa asked.

"Me? No, I am not afraid. What must be done, must be done. There is no other way. Always must a person fight. All his life. I know this."

"Don't worry about it. I will be very careful."

"Careful. Yes. I too am careful. You must be very sure."

"Don't worry, Mama Rosetti."

He rose to leave.

"You have a coat?"

"Yes. In the checkroom."

"Wrap up good," she said. "Don't catch cold."

Her black eyes followed him as he left the restaurant.

He made a routine check of the job the next morning. Baxter's office was on the West Side in a building on 56th Street. Costa arrived there a little before nine o'clock, losing himself in the crowd of incoming office employees, waiting at the end of the hall on the eleventh floor where he could see the entrance to Baxter's office. He was not pleased with the area. It was awkwardly arranged for a killing, with its manned elevators, people coming and going and too many late-hour businesses.

Baxter entered his office at nine-thirty, a dapper, squat individual, with a stub of a cigar clamped in his jaws. Costa waited another fifteen minutes in the hall, then entered the office, handing Baxter's secretary a card showing him to be the salesman for an office-supply company. He politely accepted the secretary's statement that Mr. Baxter was happy with his present supplier, and left, after a photographic glance at the interior of the office. He shook his head in dissatisfaction as he rode down in the elevator.

That afternoon he drove up to Connecticut in a rented car, stopping at a real-estate agent's office close to the second address that Rosetti had given him for Baxter. The agent obligingly drove him through the area, rattling off the virtues of life in Connecticut as she did so. His examination of the Baxter house was made easier by the presence of a vacant house a few doors away, in which he indicated great interest. At his request, the agent drove him down the street while he examined the homes of his potential neighbors. Baxter's was the last one in a group of six, an ostentatious modern facing the Sound, enclosed by a high brick wall. Costa stopped for a moment to study it. The entrance was barred by an ornamental iron gate, a large "Beware of the Dog" sign across the corner of it. In the yard beyond the gate, a large boxer set up a frantic clamor at their approach.

Costa spent the rest of the afternoon as a prospective customer, thoroughly convincing the receptive agent that he was a transplanted executive named Zweller from a small business in Ohio, that his wife would arrive shortly, and that he would be back with her to buy a house. In the process, he was given a gratuitous rundown on the goings and comings of the local homeowners, including Baxter, who was known as a widower of quiet habits, currently living alone, cared for by a Swedish couple who slept in town.

At six o'clock he was back at the Rosetti's, seated in their living room. Rosetti was planted in the chair behind his desk. Mama Rosetti across the room at her endless knitting.

"I have Mama here. Like you said on the phone."

Costa looked at the woman, then back to Rosetti. "I wanted to talk to you together," he said. "The job is possible. Only one thing about it I don't like."

"What don't you like?"

"I need a little insurance," Costa said.

Rosetti leaned toward him. "You mean you won't do it?"

"I mean I won't do it without help. I'll need you both."

Mama Rosetti folded her hands into her lap. "Make me understand," she said.

"I don't like his office for the job. Too busy. It'll have to be the house. I won't drive to it."

He paused.

"So?" Rosetti said.

"So we go fishing this weekend. All three of us. I'll tell you where to anchor. I'll take care of the assignment while we're there. That will make you both accessories before and after the fact. Makes for a nice silent relationship in the future."

Rosetti turned to the woman. "Mama?" he said.

She looked at Costa for a long moment. Then she sighed, nodding her head slowly.

"I think it is all right, Papa," she said. "It is a thing we have to do. I do not blame him for his caution."

Rosetti turned to Costa. "We will do it," he said. "We have no choice."

"We have a deal," Lee Costa said.

"What must we do?" Rosetti asked.

"Pick me up Saturday morning at the gas dock at City Island. Gas the boat. I'll come aboard while the attendant's busy." Costa rose to leave. "After that, I'll tell you where to go. Leave the rest to me."

"Wrap up good," Mama Rosetti said. "Don't catch cold."

Lost in a crowd of yachtsmen and guests, Costa was an unobtrusive figure as he waited on the public dock the following Saturday. He watched quietly while the Rosettis arrived on a small cruiser, edging it to the dock. Then he worked his way through a crowd of noisy fishermen and stepped aboard, moving into the cabin while Rosetti kept the harassed attendant busy. Minutes later, they were moving toward the Connecticut shore, Rosetti at the wheel, Costa beside him, Mama Rosetti at her endless knitting in a wicker chair.

Early in the afternoon, they anchored the boat in the sheltered area around the point of the peninsula on which the Baxter house rested.

"What now?" Rosetti asked nervously.

"Eat. Fish. Be a playboy," Costa said.

"You hungry?" Mama Rosetti asked.

"A little."

"All right, I make dinner. Now, you fish with Papa."

At six o'clock she called to them from the cabin door. "Come downstairs," she called. "We'll eat."

"Below, Mama," Rosetti said. "Not downstairs."

"Downstairs," she said. "You're the sailor. I'm the cook."

It was a tense meal, Rosetti stopping to look nervously at Costa, Mama Rosetti silent and occupied with serving them from the galley stove.

Costa rested on one of the bunks for half an hour afterwards, arising to find the questioning eyes of the Rosettis on him again. "I'm going for a little swim," he said.

Mama Rosetti reached out a small brown hand, patted his arm. "Be careful," she said.

He smiled down at her. "I'm always careful," he said. "I'm a very cautious boy."

He disappeared into the cabin, appearing a few minutes later in swimming trunks and the top half of a skindiver's wet suit. He stood for a moment near the stern, placed a black rubber hood on his head, flippers on his feet, worked mask and snorkel into place and dropped softly into the water. He checked the collar of his wet suit to be sure that the small plastic bag he had tucked there was still in place, felt for the rubber gloves attached to his belt and swam slowly toward the shore, slipping smoothly through the black water, the rubber suit and flippers giving him enough buoyancy to conserve his strength.

A half-hour later, he stopped a few feet from the end of the Baxter dock, then drifted in until he could rest his weight on the bottom. He reached again under the collar of his suit, pulled out the bag, opened it, carefully keeping the piece of meat it contained out of the water. He gave a low whistle, waiting while the dog's feet made a rhythmic thumping on the dock. He threw the meat almost at the feet of the dog, whose barking echoed along the quiet beach. Then he slipped back into deep water again, floating, head low in the water, breathing through his snorkel, head down, virtually invisible from the shore. The barking grew louder.

A moment later, the robed figure of Baxter came out onto the upstairs porch, flashlight in hand. After a careful examination of the yard, he called down to silence the dog. Costa waited.

After Baxter returned to his room, the dog nosed around the end of the dock restlessly, then turned to give his attention to the meat. Costa could see the outline of the animal as he nuzzled it, hear the ugly little sounds as he gulped it down. He waited while an agonized whine came from the dog, his frantic feet drumming on the dock. When the sound stopped, Costa floated in again, gave another low whistle. There was no reaction from the dog. Costa stuck his head up cautiously. The animal was lying near the edge of the dock. Costa pulled off the mask and flippers, then pulled the body of the dog into the shadow cast by the boathouse. A tiny portion of the meat was still on the wooden floor of the dock. Carefully, he picked it up and threw it into the sea, returning to the shadowed area to wait patiently for a long half-hour, pleased when the servants appeared at the back door on schedule to climb into a station wagon. They drove away, the gate closing automatically behind them.

Costa let the sound of the disappearing car die out before he got out of his swimming gear and moved to the balustrade of the porch. Slowly, he snaked up it, slipping over the edge of the upstairs rail soundlessly, lying on the floor of the porch a good ten minutes before he moved again. On his belly, he slipped the gloves on his hands, after which he wormed his way to the edge of the French windows. They were open. Two minutes later, he was standing over the sleeping form of Roy Baxter. Costa braced his feet. His hands fastened to the throat of the sleeping man. Costa held on for a long time, then stripped a glove from his right hand to check the pulse of the body in the bed. Satisfied that Baxter was dead, he placed the glove on his hand again and left the way he had come.

At the dock, he replaced his swimming gear, pulled the dog's body to the edge of the dock and dropped with it into the water. He stopped to estimate the direction of the Rosetti boat before he towed the dog's body well out into the Sound, releasing it where the outgoing tide would carry it away. He worked his way slowly and easily back to the boat, letting the tide aid him in the long swim. As he approached it, he could see the Rosettis sitting in the stern cockpit.

"Costa?" Rosetti called.

"Coming in," Costa said. He handed them the flippers and the mask, climbing over the edge of the cockpit almost at the feet of the Rosettis. "It's done," he said.

Mama Rosetti looked at him, her black eyes inscrutable in the soft light.

"No trouble?"

"No trouble."

"Take off those wet clothes. You freeze to death."

Costa went into the cabin, peeled out of the rubber jacket, dried his head, put on slacks and a sweater and returned to the Rosettis.

Mama Rosetti was back in her wicker chair, her hands busy again with the knitting. From somewhere Papa Rosetti had pulled out a bottle of wine.

"Here," he said to Costa, "Drink." He poured three glasses.

They drank. For a long time Mama Rosetti studied Costa's face. "Everything all right, huh?" she said.

"Worked fine," Lee Costa said. "Nobody saw me. Nobody knows I'm here. Nobody knows what happened. Except you and me."

"You shoot him?" Rosetti asked.

"I don't use guns," Costa said. "These are good enough." He held up a hard hand, pointed to the rim of calluses on the ridge of his palm.

Rosetti stood by the cabin door. "I'm tired, Mama."

She looked over at him, her face warm with concern. "Cover up good, Papa. Sleep well." She turned to Costa. "You too, Mr. Costa. You need to go to bed."

Costa rose, standing on the deck of the boat to stretch. "Nice night, isn't it?" he said, smiling down at her.

"Yes," she said, pulling an ugly little automatic out from under her knitting. "A very nice night." She shot him, twice, over the heart. Costa's body was thrown backwards, hitting the water with a soft splash. Mama Rosetti leaned over the rail of the boat, pistol in hand, while she watched the body sink, as it slowly moved away with the tide.

"What now, Mama?" Rosetti's head was sticking out of the cabin door.

She turned to him gravely. "Nothing more. It is finished." She threw the pistol over the side. "Cover up good, Papa. Don't catch cold."

SOMETHING VERY SPECIAL

by Fletcher Flora

Clara DeForest, Mrs. Jason J. DeForest, was entertaining her minister, the Reverend Mr. Kenneth Culling, who conducted himself with a kind of practiced and professional reticence, faintly suggesting a reverent hush, that was appropriate to a house of bereavement. The situation, however, was delicate. In fact, the Reverend Mr. Culling was not at all certain that his visit, under the ticklish circumstances, was quite proper. So far as he could determine, there seemed to be no etiquette established for such occasions. But he had decided he could not afford to risk offending a parishioner as prominent as Clara DeForest, and that he must offer at least a tactful expression of sympathy. So here he was, with a teacup balanced on his knee and a small sweet cracker in his hand.

It was close to the time when he customarily fortified himself with a glass of sherry, and he wished wistfully that he were, at this instant, doing that very thing. He was unaware that Clara DeForest, who was also drinking tea and eating crackers, would have greatly preferred a glass or two of sherry, and would have happily supplied it. In short, the two were not quite in contact, and they were forced to suffer, consequently, the petty misery common to misunderstandings.

Clara DeForest's bereavement, to put it bluntly, was qualified. It was true that her husband Jason was gone, but he had gone of his own volition, aboard a jet headed for Mexico City, and not in the arms of angels headed for heaven. At least, that was the rumor. It was also rumored that he had withdrawn his and Clara's joint checking account and sold some bonds, had helped himself to the most valuable pieces in Clara's jewelry box, and had been accompanied on the jet by a platinum blond. Clara made no effort to refute these charges. Neither did she confirm them. She merely made it clear, with a touch of pious stoicism, that she preferred to forgive and forget the treacheries of her errant husband, whatever they may have been precisely. Her marriage to Jason, twenty years her junior, had been under sentence from the beginning, and it was well over and done with. She was prepared, in short, to cut her losses. The Reverend Mr. Culling was vastly relieved and reassured to find her so nicely adjusted to her misfortune. "I must say, Mrs. DeForest," he said, "that you are looking remarkably well."

"I feel well, thank you."

"Is there nothing that you need? Any small comfort that I may offer?"

"I am already quite comfortable. I appreciate your kindness, but I assure you that I need nothing."

"Your fortitude is admirable. A lesser woman would indulge herself in tears and recriminations."

"Not I. The truth is, I have no regrets whatever. Jason has deserted, and I am well rid of him."

"Do you feel no resentment, no anger? It would be perfectly understandable if you did."

The Reverend Mr. Culling looked at Clara hopefully. He would have been pleased to pray for the cleansing of Clara's heart. It would have given him something to do and made him feel useful. But Clara's heart, apparently, required no cleansing. "None at all," she said. "Jason was a young scoundrel, but he was quite a charming one, and I am rather grateful to him than otherwise. He gave me three exciting years at a time of life when I had no reasonable expectation of them."

The nature of Clara's excitement took the shape of a vague vision in the minister's mind, and he tried without immediate success to divert his thoughts, which were hardly proper in connection with a woman of fifty, or any woman at all, however effectively preserved. He could not be blamed for noticing, however, that Clara was still capable of displaying a slender leg and a neat ankle.

"There are unexpected compensations," he murmured

with a vagueness equal to that of his vision.

"On the contrary, I did expect them, and I had them. I should hardly have married Jason for any other reason. He was poor. He was unscrupulous and rather stupid. He was pathetically transparent even in his attempts to kill me."

"What!" The Reverend Mr. Culling's voice escaped its discipline and jumped octaves into an expression of horror. "He made attempts on your life?"

"Twice, I believe. Once with something in a glass of warm milk he brought me at bedtime. Another time with something in my medicine. He repeated, you see, the same basic technique. Jason, like all dull young men, had absolutely no imagination."

"But surely you reported these attempts to the police!"

"Not at all. What would have been the good? It would merely have destroyed our whole relationship, which still retained from my point of view, as I have indicated, much that was satisfactory."

The minister, feeling that he was somehow on trial, tried to restrain his emotions. "Do you mean that you did nothing whatever about it?"

"Oh, I did something, all right." Clara smiled tenderly, remembering what she had done. "I simply explained that I had disposed of my small fortune in such a way as to deprive him of any motive for killing me. Since he would receive no benefits from my death, there was no advantage in trying to rush what will occur, in any event, soon enough. He was like a child. So embarrassed at being detected!"

"Like a monster, I should say!" The Reverend Mr. Culling's restraint faltered for a moment, and he rattled his teacup in his saucer to show the height of his indignation. "I must admit that your method was ingenious and effective."

"Was it? Not entirely." Clara's tender smile took on a touch of sadness. "It may have deprived him of any motive for killing me, but it also relieved him of any compelling reason for sticking around. Not, as I said, that I have regrets. At least, no serious ones. But I shall miss Jason. Yes, indeed, I shall miss him. I shall certainly keep some small momento around the house to keep my memory of him fresh and vivid. As one grows older, you know, one's memories fade without the help of mnemonics."

"He has only been gone for a week. Perhaps he'll return."

"I think not." Clara shook her head gently. "He left a note, you know, saying that he was leaving for good. Besides, he could, under the circumstances, hardly be sure of his reception. In a moment of pique, I destroyed the note. I regret now that I did. I should have kept it to read periodically. It would have served admirably to bring him back in spirit, if not in flesh."

"You are an astonishing woman, Mrs. DeForest. I am utterly overwhelmed by your incredible charity."

"Well, it is reputedly a Christian virtue, is it not?"

"Indeed it is. Faith, hope and charity, and the greatest of these . . ."

The minister's voice trailed off, not because the rest of the words had slipped his mind, but because he chose not to compete with the front doorbell, which had begun to ring. Clara DeForest, in response to the ringing, had stood up. "Excuse me," she said, and left the room.

He heard her a moment later in the hall, speaking to someone at the door. He was disturbed and a little confused by her almost placid acceptance of what he considered a shameful and faithless act. He was, in fact, inclined to resent it as an excessive application of his own principles. After all, it was entirely possible to be too understanding and submissive. His head tended to reel with antic thoughts, and he leaned back in his chair and looked for something substantial on which to anchor them. His eyes centered on a vase on the mantel, which made him think of Keats' "Ode on a Grecian Urn." Odes and urns seeming safe and substantial enough, he began trying to recall the lines of the poem, but he could only remember the famous one about a thing of beauty being a joy forever, a contention which he privately considered extravagant and dubious. Clara DeForest returned to the room. She was carrying a package wrapped in brown paper and tied with string. Placing the package on a table, she went back to her chair.

"It was the postman," she explained. "Will you have more tea?"

"No, thank you. No more for me. I was just admiring the vase on your mantel. It's a lovely thing."

"Yes, isn't it?" Clara turned her head to look at the vase, her eyes lingering. "My brother Casper brought it to me last week when he drove up to see me."

"I heard that your brother was here. It's a great comfort to have a loved one near in a time of trouble."

"Yes, Casper came immediately when I told him by telephone that Jason had left me, but it was hardly necessary. I did not consider it a time of trouble, actually, and I was perfectly all right. I suppose he merely wanted to reassure himself. He only stayed overnight. The next morning, he drove directly home again."

"I have never had the pleasure of meeting your brother. Is his home far away?"

"About two hundred miles. He lives in the resort area, you know. He's a potter by trade. He made the little vase you have been admiring."

"Really? How fascinating!"

"It's actually an art, not a trade, but Casper has developed it to the point where it is also a business. He started out years ago with a little shop where he sold his own wares, but they were so superbly done that the demand for them grew and grew, and he soon had to increase the size and numbers of his kilns to meet it. Now he supplies shops and department stores in all the larger cities of this area."

"He must be very busy."

"Oh, yes. Yes, indeed. He was forced to hurry home last week because he had some urgent work to do. He has great artistic integrity, you see. He personally makes all his own vases. It limits his production, of course, but each piece is far more valuable because of it."

"I know so little about the making of pottery. I must read up on it."

"You will find it interesting, I'm sure. The pieces are baked, for instance, in intense heat. Have you any idea of the temperature needed to produce a piece of biscuit ware?"

"Biscuit ware?"

"That is what the pottery is called after the initial baking, before glazing."

"Oh. No, I must confess I haven't the slightest idea."

"An average temperature of 1,270 degrees."

"Mercy!"

"Centigrade, that is."

"Good heavens!"

"So, you see," Clara finished humorously, "my lovely vase has been put through quite an ordeal. Don't you agree it is worth it, though? It is too squat for most flowers, of course, but never mind. I shall keep it for something very special."

Talk of such heat had prompted the Reverend Mr. Culling to think uneasily of Hell. He preferred talking of it to thinking of it, for silence increased its terrors, but it would hardly do as a topic for this polite conversation, which had continued, at any rate, long enough. He rose.

"Well, I must run along. I really must. I can't tell you how relieved I am to find you taking things so well."

"You mustn't worry about me. I'll survive, I assure you."

They walked to the front door and said goodby.

"I'm so glad you called," said Clara. "Do come again soon."

From the door, she watched him to his car at the curb, and then she turned and went back into the living room. At the table, she took up the package with an expression of annoyance. Really, Casper was simply too exasperating! It was well enough to be thrifty, but her dear brother was positively penurious. Not only was the package flimsy and insecurely tied, but it had been sent third class, just to save a few cents' postage. Of course, one realized that postal employees rarely availed themselves of the right to open and inspect packages, but just suppose, in this instance, one had! It would have been embarrassing, to say the least.

She took the lovely vase from the mantel and set it on the table beside the package. Her annoyance dissolved in a feeling of delicious companionship. Opening the package, she began to pour its contents into the vase.

THE SHORT AND SIMPLE ANNALS

by Dan J. Marlowe

I'D JUST COME OUT from under the welding hood and was inspecting a silver seam intended to staunch a leak in a battered radiator when "Fat" Carson, the welding-shop hack, touched me on the arm. "You're wanted in the warden's office, Toland," he said. He led the way to the door, unlocking it and then carefully relocking it behind us, observing the regular procedure.

We marched down the echoing stone corridor while I tried to think where I could have put my foot down wrong. I was no stranger to such summonses, but I hadn't been up before the mast in some time. Carson left me at the door of Warden Wibberly's office, and I went in and braced in front of his desk, standing stiffly at attention. To the left of the chunky, gray-haired Wibberly, a big man in a dark business suit sat off to one side. It took a second look from the corner of my eye before I recognized Tom Glick, the precinct police captain from my home town who'd sent me up. I'd never seen him out of uniform before.

"Have a chair, Toland," Wibberly said. "Smoke if you like." He actually sounded pleasant.

"Thank you, sir." I lit up quickly. You can't smoke under a welding hood. I sat at attention in the designated chair.

Wibberly opened a file folder on his desk. I knew it was mine, because one of the mug shots taken when I arrived at the prison was pasted to the outside of the tan folder. It showed a black-haired, rugged-looking type with big shoulders and a hell-to-you look in the eyes. I hadn't seen much of that look lately in my shaving mirror.

"I've been looking over your record here," Wibberly began. "Upon arrival you were close to being an incorrigible, but I note that in the past thirty months no disciplinary action has been necessary. Except for your choice of friends,

I'd say that you made a good, if belated, adjustment." I didn't say anything. I wondered what he was leading up to. Off to the side, Glick was elaborately studying the lighted tip of his cigarette.

Wibberly closed the folder, cleared his throat, and looked directly at me in my chair. "I have news for you, Toland. A professional thief named Danny Lualdi was shot and critically wounded by a policeman. Before he died, he gave the police a list of the crimes he'd committed. The Gurnik Baking Company safe job was on the list, and bullets fired from Lualdi's pistol matched the one fired at the Gurnik watchman in the getaway, and which was later removed by the police from a door. There's no question Lualdi did the job."

I could feel the old adrenalin coursing through me. I couldn't sit still; I bounced upright, pinching out my cigarette and automatically dropping the butt into my pocket. "Then where does that leave me?" I demanded. "I've done three years, two months, and seventeen days for that job on the strength of a positive identification by Spider Haines, the Gurnik night watchman."

"It leaves you a free man." Wibberly gestured at his desk. "The governor has signed a pardon for you that takes effect at noon tomorrow. When it does, you'll be walking out that gate down there." He pointed to the steel doors in the forty-foot gray wall that could be seen from his office window.

A buzzer sounded, signaling the 4:30 P.M. end of the prison work day. "In that case," I said, "if you've nothing more to say, I've got people to see and things to do."

I'd stopped saying "sir," and he'd noticed it. His mouth drew down at the corners. "Captain Glick has a word to say to you before you leave this office, Toland." Wibberly got up and left, closing the outside door behind him.

"I suppose you're already spending the money you're going to get for suing the state and the department for false arrest and imprisonment?" Glick rumbled at me.

"I hadn't had time to think of it yet, but thanks for the idea."

"Don't do it," he said. His tone was flat and unemotional.

"I'd like to see you stop me." I warmed to the subject. "I'd like to see you try. Even with a pardon, what kind of a job can I get when employers know where I've been? You bet your life I'm going to sue! Julie and the baby can use the money, too."

"Don't do it," he said again. "There are people who wouldn't like it." He rose from his chair. I'm no midget, but he outbulked me in all directions. "You're no rose, Toland. You had a previous record—"

"Misdemeanors!" I burst out. "A couple of fights . . ."

"The rap sheet says the charges were reduced from assault. And on the Gurnik job, Haines identified you."

"With you twisting his arm!"

Glick's rocklike expression never changed. "I picked up Marsh Wheeler the other day," he said. "Used to be a friend of yours, didn't he?" He was watching my face. Fear nibbled at me, sharp as a rat's teeth. "Old Marsh is going up this time. Open-and-shut case. He got careless." Glick was still watching me. "Didn't seem to be any point in it before, but maybe I ought to lean on him and ask him who his partner was in the days before you went away?" He waited, but I didn't say anything. I couldn't have said anything. Glick seemed satisfied with the impression he had created. "You're a machinist, or were," he said. "Work at it. Stay out of my sight. And forget the suing." He strolled to the door.

Wibberly reentered immediately. "All right, Toland," he said briskly. "See you tomorrow."

I got out of there, so mad I could hardly see. They thought they had me nailed down, did they? Well, I'd show them.

I had the guard who picked me up at the door take me down to the gym, where I usually went after work. Benny the Weasel Krafcik and Trigger Dunn were sitting on stools beside the lifting mat, talking. They were my closest friends in the prison—the choice of friends of which Wibberly had disapproved—but I didn't know how to break the news to them. I stripped to the waist and loosened up with the fifteen-pound dumbbells, shifted to the thirties and worked up a sweat. I hoisted a bar bell over my head a few times, then let it drop to waist level and did a few curls. It's good for the arms. I'd gone from a medium to a large size in shirts since I'd been on the weights, and I was only another layer of muscle away from extra-large.

Finally I broke into the low-pitched conversation. "I'm leaving tomorrow, fellas," I told them.

"That's too bad, Igor," Benny said. He called everyone who lifted weights Igor, his idea of a joke.

"Yeah," Trigger chimed in. "What'd you do to get yourself transferred out? An' where they shippin' you to?"

"OUT," I emphasized. "On the bricks. A pardon."

Their smiles were both quick and genuine. It's not hard —in fact, it's extremely easy—to dislike the man getting out ahead of you, but these were my friends. Benny was a safe mechanic, and a good one. Trigger was a gunman. Nobody except a few intimates called him "Trigger" to his face. Benny lifted weights, too, but not Trigger. "How strong do you have to be to pull a trigger?" he'd ask, and laugh.

"How to go, man," Benny said softly. "This change your plans any?"

"It's going to speed them up considerably."

Trigger smiled. "Hope you remember everything Benny's pounded into you," he said.

The conversation died. I couldn't think of anything to say. I knew what they were thinking: *here's a guy making it to the street. By tomorrow this time he'll be doing all the things we'd like to be doing out there*. Anything I said would be so much rubbing it in. "You sure you got it all straight?" Benny asked finally. I rattled off names, addresses, and telephone numbers. They both nodded. Benny had a few special questions. I answered them. He smiled, satisfied. The buzzer sounded for the end of the recreation period, and I exchanged a cross-handed handshake with them, both at the same time. They each said the one word: "Luck!" and we went off to our cells.

That night I wrote Julie a long letter. I told her about

the pardon. I didn't tell her I was getting out the next day; I told her I loved her and the baby. Baby? Lucy was four years old now. And I'd be seeing them the first part of the week. This first part was certainly true, and I hoped the last part was just as true.

I was processed out by one o'clock the next afternoon. The prison clothing shop outfitted me with slacks and a sport jacket that fitted reasonably well. The warden handed me my pardon, a copy of my release papers, a one-way bus ticket to the city, my wallet, and $86.14, the money I'd earned in prison. I went out through the steel gates, walked to the bus terminal, and caught the one-thirty bus, settling down in it for the ten-hour ride.

En route, during a stopover, I bought a cheap briefcase, shaving gear, a toothbrush, a shirt, and a couple of changes of underwear. I'd left all my things behind me in favor of a fresh start. The briefcase was my only luggage when we reached town. I took a cab up to the Hotel Carlyle, where no one questioned my skimpy luggage or hatless, crew-cut head. I signed the register with my right name. When they came looking for me, I wanted to make it easy for them.

Despite my late arrival, I showered and shaved. Then I went out to a nearby steakhouse and savored every bite of a $6.50 porterhouse. After strawberry shortcake and three cups of coffee, real coffee, I went to a pay phone and made two calls. Both parties assured me they'd had the word and would expect to see me the next day. I went back to the hotel, and after half an hour's tossing and turning on the strange bed, I finally fell asleep.

The first address in the morning turned out to be a barber shop in a rundown neighborhood. "I called here last night," I said to the bald-headed barber who was alone in the place. "You're Trigger's friend who just got out?"

"That's right. I'd like to borrow a .45 Colt automatic and a clip-on holster."

"Borrow? That's not what makes the world go round, mister."

"Trigger said you owed him a favor."

He shrugged, and went to the front door and bolted it.

He led me to another door in the back and up two steps into a narrow hallway that opened on what looked like an apartment in the rear. "Wait here," he said in the hallway. In five minutes he was back with the automatic, the holster, and a dozen rounds of ammunition. I wrapped the bullets in my handkerchief to keep the grease off my pants, and dropped the handkerchief in my pocket. I clipped the holster on my belt and holstered the automatic. It felt heavy, but it felt right.

Back out in the barber shop, I pointed to the large mail slot in the front door. "I'll drop these things back in here tonight," I said. "Wrapped." He opened the door and let me out.

The second stop was a cab ride across town. It was a barroom. I introduced myself to the bartender as a friend of Benny the Weasel, and he pointed out to me Benny's friend who was waiting for me. "I want to borrow Benny's vest," I told him, "and the kit. I'll return it tonight and you can put it away for him again."

"I'll bring it across the street to the diner in half an hour," he said.

He was ten minutes late. I was on my second cup of coffee when he showed. He put down a heavy, brown paper-wrapped package on the counter beside me. I hefted it. It must have weighed twenty pounds. "I'll have it back by midnight," I said.

"Good enough," he said, and took off.

In a nearby pawnshop I bought a used suitcase. At a hardware store I bought a small can of paint remover, a large sheet of heavy brown wrapping paper, and a ball of twine. I put everything into the suitcase and moved on to a drugstore. I bought two dollars' worth of stamps at a stamp machine. I added the stamps to the collection in the suitcase, and took another cab back to the hotel.

At the front desk I bummed an address label from the clerk. Up in the room I addressed the label to a fictitious address in a nearby town. In the upper left-hand corner of the label I put Julie's name and return address. When the parcel turned out to be undeliverable eventually it would be returned to Julie's apartment.

I opened up the brown paper package and examined Benny's canvas vest. It was an adjustable type, and I had to loosen the straps before it fitted snugly under my sport jacket. It had twenty-two large and small pockets, and I took a careful inventory of the contents. Everything seemed to be there. Because of a small drill motor in a pocket on the right hand side, I had to unclip my holster and refasten the pistol on my left, to avoid a suspicious bulge. With the weight of the kit distributed around the trunk of my body, I hardly felt I was carrying anything.

I looked at my watch. Two o'clock. I took off the vest and stretched out on the bed for a nap. At six I got up and put the vest back on, reclipped the holster, and buttoned the jacket over everything. I was ready to go. I wouldn't eat until after the job.

I walked the two and a half miles to Gurnik's. I had plenty of time, and no desire to test cab drivers' memories for faces in a police roundup. The bakery covered most of a block, and I came up on the rear of it, passing a mail box on the corner. The watchman's shack was just inside the four-foot stone wall, behind the closed gate. I passed it on the wrong side of the street, and I could see the white-haired Spider Haines at his desk in the shack, the same wizened Spider Haines whose testimony had sent me up.

When he left the shack on his eight o'clock rounds, I vaulted the wall. Benny's information was that Haines made a tour of the plant every two hours. At the back door of the main building I unloaded the suitcase; I put paint remover, twine, address label, and stamps in my pockets, and folded the wrapping paper and carried it under my arm. When Haines came back out the door after punching his clocks, I met him halfway through it. He took one look at the gun in my hand and another at my face and went right down on his skinny knees. "Don't do it, Toland!" he begged. "Glick *made* me testify!"

He had nothing to worry about, but he didn't know it. I wanted him very much alive. I prodded him upright with the pistol and hustled him down the corridor to where the cashier's office should be, according to Benny's information. It was there, all right, and so was the safe, a large double-door model.

I tied Haines into a chair. His eyes rolled up at me; he was shivering as though with an ague. I pulled the chair into a corner out of sight of the safe, and left him there. He wasn't about to make any noise; he had to figure he was a big winner. Besides, after sundown in that warehouse neighborhood, not even a good-sized explosion would have had an audience.

On my way to the safe I took the can of paint remover from my pocket. I opened it, and spread a four inch border of it around the upper half of the door containing the combination dial. I gave it time to soften the paint, and then scraped it off with a putty knife I took from the vest. The bare metal of the safe door was now exposed. Working quickly, I took a two-pound lead block from the vest and screwed a steel handle into it. Using it as a mallet, I struck the face of the door sharply several times. Cracks appeared around the heads of previously invisible rivets that had been machined flush with the surface of the door.

Successful safecracking requires specialized knowledge, skill with tools, and physical strength. I centerpunched each rivet, and then drilled off the head of the dial. I took the pry-bar from the vest. It consisted of four six-inch steel lengths that screwed together. One of them had been the mallet handle, and it had several interchangeable tips. I used a flat tip first to loosen the front plate, and then switched to a hook shape to bend the plate down, exposing the concrete lining. After shifting again to a pointed tip, I knocked out the concrete to get at the bolt works.

It was hot, dusty work. A fine film of cement dust settled over everything. When I had the bolt works exposed, all I had to do was remove one pin from the main bolt arm. The bolts retracted easily. The doors opened smoothly. This was no safe with another steel door behind the first one. The cash was right out in plain sight.

I scooped it out and piled it on the floor. The denominations on the packages of bills made pleasant reading.

I found some cardboard for a stiffener, made a neat stack of the whole business, and wrapped it all up in the heavy brown wrapping paper I'd brought along. I tied it securely with twine, using double knots, applied the previously prepared label and over two dollars' worth of stamps, and was ready to drop it into a mailbox. In the post office's own good and sufficient time, the package would arrive at Julie's marked RETURN TO SENDER.

I slipped out of the vest and wrapped it, too, and I made two small packages of the gun and the holster. I went over everything in the place carefully with a damp rag, erasing possible fingerprints. I didn't forget Benny's tools. With the same rag I cleaned my shoes. After brushing off my slacks, I picked up my packages and went out the way I'd come in, stopping at the back door to pick up the suitcase and take that with me, too.

I dropped the money package into the mailbox at the end of the block. The suitcase I shoved into a doorway after wiping it for prints. I walked rapidly away from Gurnik's. When Haines didn't make his ten-o'clock round, someone was going to investigate. My nerves were screaming for transportation, but I made myself walk a mile before I hailed a cab. I made my first stop the barber shop, where I pushed the wrapped pistol and holster through the mail slot. At the diner I left Benny's kit with the short order cook. Back at the Carlyle I took a long shower, dressed again, and stretched out on the bed to wait. I knew it wouldn't be long, and it wasn't.

When the pounding started on the door, I was sure it was Glick, even before I opened it. "Let's go," he ordered without preliminary.

"What's the charge this time, Captain?" I asked him. "Spitting on the sidewalk?"

He refused to answer. We rode downtown with a detective on either side of me on the back seat, and Glick glowering up front beside the driver. An Assistant District Attorney was waiting when they brought me in. "Gurnik's safe was burglarized tonight, and the watchman says you did it," he started in on me. "You must be out of your mind, even if you think you did get a bum rap before. Now, if you turn over the money and make a full statement, I'm sure the judge will take it into consideration when he hears all the facts in the case."

I laughed in his face. "Mister Whatever-Your-Name-Is, I don't know what happened at Gurnik's, if anything did, but I'll tell you something. Spider Haines' testimony will never convict anyone again, let alone me. Didn't he already identify me once in error? You think a jury's going to believe him again?"

It wasn't that easy, of course. There was browbeating and breast-beating, and telephone calls, and hurried, whispered consultations. They rushed me from room to room, fingerprinting me, and taking my picture. And at 2:00 A.M. they gave up and threw me out on the street. Glick's face was like a thundercloud. I walked along, laughing to myself. It was beautiful, just beautiful. I'd really put it over on them. All I needed now was to get rid of the load of tension that had built up in my stomach like a tight, hard ball. I ducked into a bar for a couple of quick ones, liquid tranquilizers.

I had three. I felt fine. I ordered a roast-beef sandwich. I'd forgotten I hadn't eaten, and I was ravenous. I could feel the tension oozing away, and being replaced by a wonderfully expansive feeling. I counted my money. I wouldn't have much left after settling up at the hotel, but Julie wouldn't mind the drought before the payoff. It would take me a while to catch up on home living. I was looking forward to it. I didn't expect to mind a bit, waiting for the package to be returned by the post office.

I cabbed back to the Carlyle and went up in the elevator. I'd check out in the morning, but first I needed a good night's sleep. At the room I had trouble with the key in the lock, and for a second I wondered if Glick had turned nasty and ordered the lock plugged to keep me out. Then the door opened and I walked in. I couldn't believe my eyes when I saw Glick inside my room. With him was a big sergeant and a bigger patrolman, and an assistant manager-looking type with a passkey. "An afterthought," Glick said, moving between me and the door. "Sergeant Bonar here is going to take a specimen of the dirt under your fingernails to see if any of it matches the cement dust down at Gurniks. So hold out your hands." The long hot shower should have taken care of that, I thought hopefully.

"And he's going to vacuum the cuffs of your slacks," Glick continued.

All I could think of was the fine layer of powdery dust filming everything in front of the Gurnik safe.

It must have been the three drinks that made me bolt for the door. I tried to run right over Glick. The next thing I knew, I was on the floor, looking up at him from my back. "Put your little vacuum on him, Sergeant," he was saying. I heard the bzz-bzz-bzz of a small electric motor. "Looks fine," Glick announced. "Mooney, you can babysit with our friend here, while I check this out. When the rest of them left, Mooney and I sat there like two bumps on a log.

After awhile the phone rang, and I took another ride downtown.

They're still after me about the money. I haven't told them anything, and I won't. I'm sure of that.

The insurance company is making the most noise. The district attorney's office is embarrassed by the newspaper publicity going back to the first Gurnik safe job, and they'd like to forget the whole thing. They as much as said that, if I'd come up with the cash, they'd see to it I was eased out the back door of wherever I was sent as soon as the headlines died down.

But there's Julie and the baby. I'm a real loser now. When I get out, I'll be good only for more of the same, or the ash heap. Either way, it doesn't leave much for them.

So I'm leaving it up to Julie.

When the package is returned, she'll know where it came from. If she wants to return it, and get me a lessened sentence, that's fine. If she doesn't, that's all right, too. She doesn't owe me anything except one small vow, and I figure I tarnished the brass on that a good while ago.

If I don't hear anything in another week, I'll be pretty sure of the answer.

OTHERS DEAL IN DEATH

by August Derleth

JUSTICE," said Solar Pons, as we sat on either side of the fire in our lodgings one misty November evening, "is a comparatively rare commodity, perhaps because it is so difficult of definition. I daresay, therefore, it is altogether fitting that one of His Majesty's magistrates should be uneasy in mind. Tell me, Parker, does the name Fielding Anstruther mean anything to you?"

"I can't say that it does," I answered after a moment's thought.

"It was a chance in a thousand you might have seen the name in the lists appended to some of those ridiculous petitions for the abolition of capital punishment—which come up from time to time. Anstruther is a magistrate in the West country, and it would appear, unless his daughter is in error, that he is very much disturbed. This came for me half an hour before your arrival."

So saying, he reached into the pocket of his dressing gown and tossed an envelope to me.

I unfolded the letter inside and read it.

Dear Mr. Pons,

As I am visiting in London for a few days I am taking the liberty of addressing you to learn whether I may call to discuss my father's trouble. He is Mr. Fielding Anstruther, magistrate at Ross, and I fear the curious events following the assizes have upset him most grievously. If the messenger fails to bring me an adverse response, I will expect to call at No. 7B at eight o'clock this evening.

I am, sir, yours respectfully,
Violet Anstruther.

I looked up. "This is surely an intriguing little note."

"Isn't it?" agreed Pons. "And one would have expected that the curious events to which Miss Anstruther refers might have achieved some public notice. But search as I may, I find little in the columns of the newspapers to suggest what it is that troubles the honorable magistrate. Save, perhaps, this little item from the *News of the World* published a week ago."

He picked up the newspaper from beside his chair and read:

> DEATH OF PERCY DIXON. Percy Dixon was found dead this morning at Ross, Hereford. Mr. Dixon had recently been charged in the matter of Henry Archer, who was the victim of foul play six months ago in his place of business in Ross. Dixon was discharged because of insufficient evidence. He appeared before Mr. Justice Anstruther.

"There is surely nothing curious about that," I said.

"Nevertheless," said Pons, "I find it interesting."

"Our client's letter mentions 'events'—so these must have been plural."

Pons glanced at the clock on the mantel. "It lacks but a few minutes of eight, and I fancy we shall have to abate our curiosity until that hour."

He filled his clay pipe with the abominable shag he smoked and settled back to wait. But he had hardly done so, when there was a ring of the outer bell, and within a few moments Mrs. Johnson showed in a young lady in her late twenties. Our visitor had a fine figure, challenging black eyes, and a provocative mouth.

"Mr. Pons," she said, as though addressing both of us, "I am Violet Anstruther."

"Come in, Miss Anstruther. Dr. Parker and I have been awaiting you."

I had got up to draw forward a chair for the woman. She thanked me and sat down as she loosened the fur piece about her neck. She betrayed a certain agitation only in the nervous way in which she clenched and unclenched her hands.

"I am at my wits' end, Mr. Pons," she began, "and I am sure that if my father knew I had come, he would be furious. He is a very reserved and proud man—very sure of himself within his world, which is that of law and justice—and certain matters would seem to have conspired to unsettle him."

"You mentioned 'certain events' in your note, Miss Anstruther, and now you again speak of them. Has your father spoken to you concerning—"

"No, Mr. Pons. Excuse me for interrupting. That is the problem. For some months now father has paced the floor long hours in the night. His appetite has fallen off. He cannot seem to sleep, yet he looks dreadfully tired. He is often so preoccupied that he is sometimes not aware that we have spoken to him."

"We?"

"My Aunt Susan, father's younger sister, lives with us." She went on, "He has lost weight, and makes some little joke or other when I call his preoccupation to his attention. Of what is on his mind, he has not said a word. I've not asked him directly, but I know if he had any intention of speaking, he would do so.

"Mr. Pons, I thought at first that perhaps money matters were at the root of his trouble. But this is not so. I have assured myself of that. His investments are sound, and our income hasn't fallen off in the least. We're comfortably situated; at mother's death, she left a considerable sum. Nor could I find any variation in his daily habits, other than those I've just mentioned, that would suggest some important alteration in his personal life. He has received no unusual mail; no one, other than the customary companions of his lifetime, has called upon him. And so, Mr. Pons, I can think of nothing but that he is concerned over the way in which some of his cases have been disposed of, post-trial, so to speak."

"Ah, then Mr. Dixon is not the only gentleman who has appeared before your father to have subsequently died?" put in Pons.

"No, sir. He is only the most recent. He is the third, altogether. The first was Hester Spring. It seems probable that she smothered her baby. My father is a very just, upright man, and he felt there was a possibility of accident. He virtually directed a verdict for acquittal. She died about a month after her discharge. The coroner's jury decided that her death was an accident; she had been drinking and smothered in her bed."

"And the next?"

"The second was Algy Foster. He ran down old Mr. Carter one night eight months ago. He served four months and paid a fine, too. He died in an accident—run over one night when he stepped out of his yard to walk up the street toward the pub. The driver of the car was never found."

"And Mr. Dixon?"

"That was apparently something to do with his heart, Mr. Pons."

"What of the matter in which he was charged?"

"Mr. Archer was held up and robbed in his shop. He seems to have put up some resistance and was brutally struck on the head. He died in the hospital a day later, as a result of this blow. The general feeling in Ross is that Dixon did it, but my father felt that the case was not proven, and again directed a verdict of acquittal. I know it sounds typically like a woman's reasoning, Mr. Pons, but I've looked everywhere else for something to fix upon, and I can come up with nothing other than these— But they are simply coincidences."

"Are they?" asked Pons. "I wonder." He was thoughtful for a moment, then asked, "These events were consecutive as you narrated them?"

Our client hesitated briefly. "Yes, Mr. Pons."

"I noticed that you hesitated, Miss Anstruther."

"That is to say, Hester Spring, Algy Foster, and Percy Dixon died in that order. Actually, though, Dixon's case was first in order before my father—then Foster, then Spring."

Pons sat for a moment in deep thought, while our client preserved a respectful silence, intently watching Pons' lean face as he sat with eyes closed, contemplating what she had told him. Presently he opened his eyes and gazed soberly at Miss Anstruther.

"These little coincidences have all taken place in Ross?" he asked.

"Yes, Mr. Pons."

"Yet Mr. Justice Anstruther sits elsewhere in the assizes? Does he?"

"Yes, of course, Mr. Pons."

"And have these coincidences dogged his decisions elsewhere?"

"Not to my knowledge."

"Curious," murmured Pons. "Most curious."

"Mr. Pons, will you look into the matter for me?"

"I confess my interest in what you have told me, Miss Anstruther," said Pons, "but if your father is determined to lock his trouble inside him, it may be difficult to approach him."

"Father sits tomorrow at Ross. It is the case of a wife beater, and father will have little sympathy for him. I propose to invite you and Dr. Parker—if he will come—" (here she smiled very prettily in my direction)—"to be my guests at dinner in our home so that you may see father for yourself. If you have no objection, since father may know your name, I propose to introduce you as—let us say, Professor Moriarty of King's College."

Pons smiled. He got to his feet and said, "Fine. Splendid."

"Paddington in the morning, Mr. Pons. The train will bring you to Ross by late afternoon. I myself leave by the last train tonight."

After she had taken her leave, Pons returned to the fireside and sat for a long time in thoughtful silence, his eyes closed, his fine, lean fingers tented before him. Presently, he glanced over at me and spoke.

"What do you make of it, Parker?"

"God disposes in His mysterious ways," I said. "It may sound trite, Pons, but that seems to me the long and short of it."

"Oh, but even He may have a little help now and then," said Pons.

"Pons, you aren't serious!" I protested. "This is surely nothing more than a series of coincidences."

"I have not said it is other than that," said Pons amiably. "I fancy that far more than three people escaped justice at Mr. Anstruther's hands, because of his horror of wrongly punishing anyone, and that they are all in good health."

"Well, that is a very sensible conclusion."

"I hope I may always be, as you put it, 'sensible,'" responded Pons, with a wry smile. "But perhaps Mr. Justice Anstruther does not think the author of these events is Providence."

"I have often found that judges tend, after a long term, to equate themselves with Providence."

Pons smiled. "It's idle to speculate about the matter. We have too few facts. If your wife can spare you, please give me the pleasure of your company tomorrow."

Late the following afternoon we crossed the lovely Severn and were soon entering Ross, a country town above the left bank of the Wye, and one little spoiled by industrialization. Our client herself waited for us at the station.

She seemed completely recovered from her agitation of the previous evening, as she announced that she had taken rooms for us at the Swan and added, "Nothing has changed at home, Mr. Pons. But you'll see for yourself when you meet father at dinner tonight."

"I look forward to it, Miss Anstruther."

Our client drove us to the Swan, where we left our valises. Then we went around to her home on the far edge of the village. It was a gracious Victorian house, surrounded by a hedge.

"For the time being," explained Miss Anstruther as she led us into the house, "we are quite alone except for the cook, who is preparing dinner. Aunt Susan spends a few hours every afternoon assisting at the local hospital—she has had some nurse's training—and the two of us take turns at the typescripts of my father's notes and papers."

"These no doubt include the records of his cases," said Pons.

"Yes—and of course, lectures he often gives, and letters to the press—he feels very strongly opposed to capital punishment, Mr. Pons."

"I was aware that he is," said Pons. "I hope you will not take it amiss if I seek to draw him out on the subject at dinner."

"By no means. It is perhaps the only subject that will stir him from his preoccupation."

Pons' glance now lingered on what was obviously a man's easychair, with a little rack of books beside it and one open on its arm, turned face down. I looked at its title —*Somnambulism and Its Causes*—and observed three other books on the rack on similar subjects.

Noticing our interest, our client said, "That is where father spends much of the night, when he is not pacing the floor. Mr. Pons, do you think you can help him?"

"We shall see."

We had not long to wait for the arrival of the other members of the household. As it happened, they came together in the car driven by our client's aunt, who had driven around to court to give her brother a lift. He appeared to be a man not much over fifty, and she perhaps not quite ten years younger. They were rather dour-faced people, clearly brother and sister, and their features had a curiously equine appearance, being long and rather more broad than average, with firm, almost prognathous jaws, wide mouths, and clear, direct eyes.

"Professor Moriarty?" repeated the magistrate, after the introduction. "Sir, that is a familiar name. What is your field?"

"Sociology," replied Pons, with a perfectly straight face.

"I am in a very real sense a student of my fellowman."

"The proper study of man," agreed Anstruther, "is, of course, man."

Our client called us to the table for dinner as Pons and Anstruther were talking.

As we sat down, Pons continued, "And you, sir, have you not made a name for yourself in your efforts to make capital punishment obsolete?"

The magistrate seemed mildly pleased. "Yes, if I may say so," he said.

"Does it not occur to you that this objective of yours may be a trifle unnatural?"

Anstruther frowned. "In what way, Professor?"

"Why, sir," said Pons, obviously enjoying himself, "surely it must have struck you that the whole matter is against nature. You would have us preserve the unfit at the expense of the fit, decades after Mr. Darwin pointed out that in nature only the fit survive to best perpetuate the species."

"That is certainly a novel idea," said Miss Susan Anstruther. "I had never thought of it that way."

"Hardly novel," said Pons. "It's only the broad view. I've always found that opponents of capital punishment, devotees of correctional treatment over punitive action, and the like, are incapable of seeing the forest for the tree—for the sake of one human being, they are quite willing to ruin society." He turned again toward our host. "Does this strike you as heresy, Mr. Anstruther?"

"I suppose," said the magistrate with a fine edge of sarcasm, "It is what you might call evolutionary."

"Touché!" cried Pons, smiling. "And what do you call your view?"

"I am a simple humanitarian, Professor."

"Ah, yes," said Pons, resuming the attack with spirit, "I have never known it to fail but that every one of these theorists—call them welfare workers or psychoanalysts or even sociologists—would have us believe theirs is the humanitarian view and any other is brutalization of the finer instincts of mankind. They are all perfectly willing to consign half a dozen worthy human beings to the grave, if they can 'rehabilitate'—I believe they call it—one lost sheep who would have left society somewhat richer if he had been quietly executed without delay in the first place."

Our host was plainly astounded, if not outraged. "Sir, that is a medieval view!"

"Another catchword. Another label," said Pons. "Mr. Justice Anstruther, I put it to you that the essential fabric of society would be vastly improved if we could liquidate a basic ten percent of mankind without quibbling over these purely false moral issues."

"Professor, that is monstrous," cried the magistrate in tones of horror. "I cannot believe you are serious."

"I was never more so," said Pons.

Our client was by now betraying some agitation, and Miss Susan Anstruther listened with quizzical interest gleaming in her eyes.

If Pons had set out to outrage our host, he could have taken no other course with equal success. Justice Anstruther was almost purple with supressed anger; he had not lifted a morsel of food to his lips since Pons' position had come clear to him, but he was too much the gentleman to forget his place as our host and could not vent the anger he manifestly felt. Pons, however, had achieved his goal, and he now spoke in more mollifying tones.

"But at least you, sir, practice what you believe. Your court has a reputation for leniency."

Mr. Justice Anstruther swallowed. "I try to be fair, sir."

"My brother gives every consideration to the accused," said Miss Susan Anstruther primly.

"And none to the victim," said Pons, chuckling. "An all too human trait. One does not see before one what is safely in the grave."

I thought Mr. Justice Anstruther would burst with fury. I put in quickly, "In my profession, too, we prefer to save lives—not destroy them."

Our client looked from Pons to me, from me to her father and back to Pons. She no more than I knew what Pons was about, but she shared my hope that Pons would soon drop the subject. Quite as if he had read our minds, Pons abruptly did so.

"Our positions are patently not reconcilable, sir," he said quietly, "and perhaps I have not given this matter as much thought as it needs. Of late, too, I have been much engaged in the study of somnambulism. Tell me, sir, do you ever walk in your sleep?"

The effect of this simple question upon our host was positively astounding. The angry red and purple washed out of his face as if a drain had been opened to draw these mottled colors away. Mr Justice Anstruther went deadly pale; his fork clattered to the table; his eyes fixed on Pons as if he looked upon a ghost.

I leaped up. "Sir, you are unwell!"

He shook his head, not trusting himself to speak. Slowly he pushed his chair back from the table. Our client flashed Pons a glance of mingled dismay and perplexity as she went around to assist her father.

Mr. Justice Anstruther came slowly to his feet, regaining his dignity. He bowed formally. "Pray excuse me, gentlemen."

Then he walked steadily from the room, our client following him.

Miss Susan Anstruther also arose, somewhat disturbed, and reproachful in her manner. She intended leaving the room, but Pons was not yet ready to let her go.

"Unless I am very much mistaken, Miss Anstruther," he said, "I believe your views do not exactly coincide with your brother's."

Miss Anstruther looked at him for a moment before replying. Then she said, "I'm not entirely in agreement with Fielding, Mr. Pons. It troubles me sometimes that there are so many who get away—completely free, on what appears to me to be technicalities. But then, I have no training in the law—as my brother reminds me when sometimes I try to talk to him about his cases."

"He resents your difference of opinion? Or your expression of it?"

She shook her head. "No, I would not say so. He only

reminds me, gently, that it is he who is the justice—not I. And he tells me women are easily upset—as I was about Henry, who was my friend—a very dear friend." Here her eyes grew misty with sudden tears, and her manner became agitated. "Fielding just lets them go." But she controlled herself and added quietly, "If you'll excuse me—it's time for me to go to church."

Pons and I both rose as she went out.

Now that we were alone, I could no longer hold back the way I felt. "In all the years I've known you, Pons," I said, "I've seldom witnessed anything more disgraceful than your conduct this evening."

He merely nodded, smiling smugly.

"How can you sit there so calmly and admit it?"

"Because it is perfectly true," he said.

At this point, Miss Violet Anstruther came back into the room, her eyes flashing, her hands clenched.

Pons was equal to the occasion. "Forgive me, Miss Anstruther," he said. "I must apologize for what must have seemed to you an inexcusable display of bad manners. But I trust you have seen that it had its *raison d'être*. Your poor father, for all his convictions, has all along had some doubts about certain of the cases up before him, and, since the hand of Providence seems to have made other disposition of his discharges, he has become obsessed with the conviction that he himself has been the instrument of Providence as he walks in his sleep.

"I observed as I came in this afternoon that your father was reading books about somnambulism and ventured a shot in the dark; it struck the bull's-eye."

Our client sank down into her chair, bewildered. "Mr Pons, I am dreadfully upset. I fail to see that you have resolved my father's doubts. You have—actually—intensified them."

"My dear young lady, I have only begun to look into the matter. And now, if you will excuse us, I wish to continue my investigation elsewhere."

Miss Anstruther hurried to the vestibule where she had hung our coats.

Pons paused at the door. "By the way, has your father ever left the house at night, to your knowledge?"

Miss Anstruther's face paled a little. "I believe he did go outside once or twice."

Pons nodded, satisfied. "Your aunt left us for church," he said then. "I take it there are evening services?"

"Not always, Mr. Pons. My aunt is a retiring sort of woman. She spends much of her time in charities, hospital work, and in church.

Still Pons lingered. "I daresay the inquest on Mr. Dixon will have been held by this time."

"Yes, Mr. Pons."

"Can you give me the coroner's name?"

"Dr. Allan Kirton, King's Head Road. I could drive you there, Mr. Pons, if you wish."

"We'll walk or take a cab. Thank you, Miss Anstruther. I believe you should be at your father's call. Do not hesitate to reveal our little deception to him if he should question you."

Once we were out of earshot of the house, I said, "Pons, this is incredible. It is hardly likely that a man with Anstruther's convictions, should have such deep-seated doubts that he would commit murder in the fantastic way you suggest."

"You're a medical man, Parker. Can you deny the possibility of such somnambulistic action?"

"Such things have happened," I was forced to admit. "But it is a well-known truth that no man asleep would perform any act which is against his nature to do when he is awake."

"I am not adequately acquainted with Mr. Justice Anstruther's nature," said Pons dryly, and didn't say another word after that until we presented ourselves to Dr. Allan Kirton.

The coroner was a cheerful little man, pink-cheeked, white-haired, and voluble.

"I certainly never expected to see Mr. Solar Pons in Ross," he said, bustling us into his house.

"A little challenge has been put to me here, Doctor," explained Pons. "I am interested in Percy Dixon."

"Dixon was a scoundrel."

"He died a natural death?"

"He did. We found heart failure."

"No suggestion of violence?"

"Not a mark on him, other than what you'd expect."

"And what would one expect, Dr. Kirton?"

"Well, Mr. Pons, he'd been in the hospital for a day or two, and naturally there was the mark of a hypodermic injection."

"Only one?"

"Only one."

"I take it you had the hospital chart for the inquest?"

Dr. Kirton smiled. "I still have it here, Mr. Pons. Would you like to see it?"

"If I may."

He bounced out of his chair, went into an inner room, and returned with the chart in question. He handed it to Pons, who studied it with narrowed, thoughtful eyes.

"Hm! Blood pressure, 178/101. A trifle high."

"A bit," said Kirton. "But consistent with his situation. He had been found unconscious in the street. They thought, of course, he'd been taken suddenly ill." The coroner chuckled.

"Pulse, 48. Low. Respiration difficult. Oxygen and ice pack."

"He was only drunk, Mr. Pons. As I told you, the fellow was a scoundrel. No wonder his heart gave out."

Pons handed the chart to me. It represented nothing but the standard treatment for anyone brought into a hospital unconscious, with irregular respiration, pulse and blood pressure.

"You held the inquest on Hester Spring?" asked Pons then.

"Of course, Mr. Pons," said Kirton. "A clear case of suffocation. Ironic, too. That was the way her baby died. She was cleared of that, but chiefly because of Anstruther's softness."

"I take it there was no suspicion of foul play?"

Kirton shook his head vigorously. "Absolutely none. There was a complete absence of any motive."

"I see."

"I'm afraid you're on a wild-goose chase, Mr. Pons," said Kirton cheerfully. "Open-and-shut cases, both of them. Open-and-shut. Both inquests were purely routine matters. Oh, carefully done, sir—I saw to that. But routine, just routine."

At the Swan, half an hour later, Pons made himself comfortable and then said, "You noticed nothing unusual about the hospital chart on Dixon?"

"Nothing," I said. "The treatment was standard. I looked in vain for evidence that he might have fallen—contusion, bruise, something of that sort; but since there was none, he plainly did not hurt himself when he fell."

"Otherwise, nothing?"

"Oh, come, Pons—I've read thousands of hospital charts."

"All the more reason for studying each with care," said Pons, with that infuriating air of having observed something that had escaped me, which was ridiculous, because I had looked over the Dixon chart with such care that I could have recited it from beginning to end if called upon to do so.

He subsided into silence.

"An interesting problem," he, finally, said, "I shall regret leaving it."

"Ah-ha! then it was as I said," I could not help pointing out. "I think, Pons, before you go, you ought to apologize to Mr. Justice Anstruther."

"I intend to do so," replied Pons. "No later than tomorrow after breakfast. In the meantime, while you sleep, I shall go out into Ross and look about a bit more."

Early the next morning, we went to the home of our client. She herself answered the door. At sight of us, her left hand flew to her lips, as if to prevent an outcry.

"Good morning, Miss Anstruther," said Pons. "I trust your father is still at home?"

"He is, Mr. Pons. He's at breakfast with Aunt Susan."

"Good, good! I should like to speak to him at once. Have you disclosed our little deception?"

"No, sir. I lacked the courage."

"It doesn't matter."

She stood aside reluctantly. Pons, however, headed directly for the dining room.

Our host of the previous evening looked his astonishment at the sight of us. He would have come to his feet, had not Pons spoken.

"Please remain seated, Mr. Anstruther. I have come primarily to offer my apologies for my conduct at dinner last night."

"I am sure, Professor—" began the magistrate stiffly.

"Sir, my name is not Moriarty," interrupted Pons. "It is Solar Pons. And I am not even a professor."

My friend's name was evidently familiar to Mr. Justice Anstruther, for, though his face paled at Pons' disclosure, his apprehension now gave way to a strange air of resignation.

"So it has come, Mr. Pons," he said quietly.

"Yes, sir. But hardly, I'm sure, as you expected."

"A police inquiry?"

"A private investigation."

"They *were* murdered!"

"I have reason to believe so. But not by a man who might have walked in his sleep! You should discipline your conscience, sir. There might have been more murders—for they are technically that, even though they were conceived as executions—save that other potential victims were simply not available to the murderer. And there is, too, the suggestion that the complusion toward murder had been satisfied with the death of the one person the murderer desired to see punished.

"The murderer had to be someone thoroughly familiar with the cases before you, with access to data perhaps not wholly available through the press or even in the course of the trials. It had to be someone who could slip into Hester Spring's house beside the church—or who could follow or accompany her in when Spring was intoxicated and smother her when she was too addled to save herself—someone who could bide his time and run down Algy Foster, or who could do it on impulse after long design when the opportunity presented itself—someone who could pump a bubble of air into a man's veins without suspicion.

"A nurse," said our client.

"And last night, after learning that she was on duty at the hospital just before Percy Dixon was discharged, I took the liberty of making a close scrutiny of your sister's car—"

"Not Susan!" cried Anstruther.

Our client pressed a hand across her lips.

Miss Susan Anstruther only looked at Pons with a contemptuous smile. "Those indentations on my car could have been made in many ways, Mr. Pons," she said. "And an embolism is hardly traceable. I'm afraid you would be spoken to severely if you came before my brother with such evidence, and he'd direct a verdict of acquittal. Isn't that true, Fielding?"

Mr. Justice Anstruther was speechless as he stared at his sister with an expression of absolute horror on his face. Our client, too, listened as if she could not believe the charge Pons had made.

"Miss Anstruther," said Pons quietly, "I have the evidence."

She turned to him. "Have you? Have you enough to convince my brother, Mr. Pons—even though he couldn't sit on the case? I doubt it. Even now he is unconvinced that they deserved to die."

"That is God's decision," burst forth Justice Anstruther.

"But *you* made it," she cried.

"I spared their lives," he answered. "And you—you took them!"

"Not proven—so far," said Miss Susan Anstruther. "And I don't think Mr. Pons has any intention of going into court with such a mass of theory unsupported by sufficient fact, or he would never have come here with his story. Isn't that so, Mr. Pons?"

"There would appear to be another way to dispose of the matter."

"Commitment," said Justice Anstruther. "It can be arranged."

"Oh, no!" cried our client.

"Dear Violet would rather have a sensational trial," said the older woman. "There are more madmen outside institutions than there are in. And now Henry's gone—"

"Henry?" repeated Anstruther.

"Henry Archer—Dixon's victim," said Pons. "Miss Susan's 'very dear friend'—whose death fired your sister's zeal to become a public executioner."

Miss Susan Anstruther smiled bitterly.

"Sister! Sister! What have you done?" murmured Justice Anstruther.

Pons took out his watch. "If you will excuse us, we have just time to catch our train."

In our compartment, while the train sped toward London, Pons spoke of my failure.

"It was not, you see, what *was* on the hospital chart that was important—but what *was not*. The coroner distinctly mentioned having observed the mark of a hypodermic injection. Yet no record of such an injection appeared on the chart. One could hardly have expected Miss Susan to set down: 'One bubble of air, intravenously injected,' could one?

"Anyone might have had the opportunity to kill these three, but why then were other cases left untroubled if not because whoever did act in these three had more ready access to them than to others? Furthermore, Mr. Justice Anstruther sat in places other than Ross; yet it was only in Ross that Providence seemed inclined to interfere with his disposition of his cases. Access was thus of prime importance.

"Miss Spring's house stood beside the church Miss Susan frequented. Miss Susan worked in the hospital to which Percy Dixon was admitted. Algy Foster's death might have been the result of sudden impulse—or it might have been planned. I believe it was done on impulse, because premeditation would have meant that Miss Susan would have had to watch Foster's place, and that might have made her conspicuous and thus directed suspicion to her. Perhaps Mr. Justice Anstruther's fear of his own sleepwalking was only a blind to prevent himself from seeing what his sister did—for he certainly knew that she disagreed vehemently with his concept of justice.

"The whole matter, however, was elementary, if different. The only possible motive for altering the court's decision to a fatal disposal of the cases seemed to be a compulsion to exact justice as the murderer conceived it. Such a compulsion rises easily in many of us when justice seems to go awry, but those who feel it seldom act upon it. Miss Susan Anstruther must have known it for many years, but it took the murder of Henry Archer to drive her to action. What we shall never know is this—did she kill out of pure complusion?—or were the executions of Spring and Foster planned to conceal the death of Dixon, for which there existed a possible motive in her friendship—or romance—with Archer?"

He shrugged. "This little matter would suggest a moral—that if too many people insist upon playing God by giving unwarranted life, it may eventually stimulate others to deal in death."

THE PROMOTION

by Richard Deming

ALTHOUGH my brother-in-law held only the title of assistant vice-president, he was the top local bank official. The Foster National Bank of Midway City was merely a branch of a large banking chain, and none of the branch managers, even in the big city banks, held higher title than vice-president.

Arnold Strong and I got along a lot better when my sister was alive, because I was Marie's pet and he didn't like to offend her. He got me my job at the bank, he loaned me a few bucks when I needed it, and he even covered for me the first time I was a couple of hundred short in my accounts.

A blistering lecture accompanied the coverup, but I didn't get fired. He replaced the money out of his own pocket and accepted my promise that I would never again touch bank funds. Then he dropped the matter until the second time I was short.

In the meantime he had become a widower and no longer had to worry about what Marie thought. I was only short a lousy seventy-five bucks this time, but you would have thought it was a million. He fired me on the spot, gave me twenty-four hours to return the seventy-five, and said he would have me jailed for embezzlement if I didn't come up with it. I had to borrow the money from a loan shark.

He really did me a favor by canning me, because I got a better job. Harry Kuntz, the bookie whose loose credit system had been the cause of both shortages, steered me to Big Joe Wurtz. Big Joe was in the business of transporting and disposing of hot merchandise from hijacked trucks and needed a driver. I got the job at two hundred a week and held it for two years, until the Feds caught one of Big Joe's trunks full of hot goods. Fortunately neither the Feds nor the state cops got to me, so the only penalty I suffered was loss of employment.

I was beginning to run low on cash when I bumped into Arnold for the first time since he'd fired me. It was at a joint about ten miles out of town called the Tom-Tom. It wasn't the sort of place you would expect to find a respected bank official. It was one of those places where the waitresses carry pencil flashlights in case anyone wants to see a menu. This didn't happen often, since people seldom went there to dine. The clientele was strictly male, and the men went there to cuddle in booths with the B-girls who worked there. For a fee, the management had no objection to customers walking out with its employees.

Although the interior of the Tom-Tom was too dark for you to recognize anyone more than two feet away, the outside was well lighted. It was about ten P.M. when I got there, and the front door opened just as I reached it.

An attractive but brittle-looking brunette of about thirty stepped outdoors. She wore an imitation muskrat stole over a skin-tight green dress, pancake makeup, thick mascara and heavy eye shadow. I recognize her as one of the Tom-Tom's veteran B-girls.

Right behind her came a thick-set, dignified-looking man of about forty-five. I halted in astonishment when I recognized him also.

"Hello, Arnold," I said.

Both he and the woman paused. I may have imagined the flush on his face, because his voice wasn't in the least embarrassed.

"How are you, Mel?" he asked.

"Fine." I smiled at the woman.

"This is Miss Tina Crawford," he said. "Tiny, my brother-in-law, Melvin Hall.

Her eyes showed recognition. We had never had a booth session together inside, but she had approached me at the bar a couple of times, and I'm not hard to remember. I'm six feet one and still in pretty good physical shape for a man pushing forty.

"I believe we've met," she said in a voice as metallic as her appearance.

"Uh-huh," I said, "How are you, Tina?"

She said she was fine and the two of them moved on. I stood gazing after them curiously until they rounded the corner of the building to the parking lot on that side. The thought of my staid brother-in-law beginning to sow some wild oats after two and a half years as a sedate widower rather tickled me.

Suddenly it occurred to me that the Foster National Bank's board of trustees undoubtedly would disapprove of one of its branch managers running around with a B-girl. A hint to that effect might induce my brother-in-law to approve a small personal loan.

There was parking space on both sides of the building, and my car was parked in the opposite direction from which Arnold and Tina had gone. Changing my mind about entering the Tom-Tom, I hustled back to my car.

A blue sedan appeared from the opposite side of the building. By the glare of the floodlight over the roadhouse's front door I could clearly see Tina and Arnold in the front seat. The car swung right, away from town, when it nosed out into the highway.

I let it get fifty yards ahead, then followed.

Arnold drove another fifteen miles away from town before swinging off on a gravel road. I was becoming more intrigued by the minute, because I knew the road. After passing a couple of farms, it came to a dead end in the middle of an isolated wooded section. Nestled in the trees at the end of the road was a huge, two-story building known as the Thirty-three Club. Its downstairs was a legitimate nightclub, the upstairs held an illegal gambling casino.

By the time I drove between the stone pillars at the entrance to the grounds, Arnold had already parked and had escorted Tina inside. I drove around the lot until I spotted his car, then found a spot in the second row behind it, where a row of cars would screen me, yet I could keep my eye on it. I waited in my car for five minutes, then went inside.

The place was crowded enough so that no one paid any attention to me when I made a circuit of the ballroom. Arnold and Tina weren't there, and neither were they in the bar. As there were no other rooms on the first floor except for the kitchen, it followed that they must have gone straight upstairs to the casino.

Arnold's board of trustees wouldn't approve of him frequenting a gambling casino any more than they would approve of him dating a B-girl, I thought. Mentally I upped the amount of the loan for which I intended to ask.

I went back out to my car and waited.

It was twelve-thirty when Arnold and Tina emerged. I gave the sedan fifty yards again, then followed. Arnold drove straight back to town and turned into the driveway of his own house.

I parked across the street and watched him close the garage doors, then lead Tina to the side door of his house and unlock it. They disappeared inside.

As Arnold and Marie had never had any children, he now occupied the house alone, and there was no reason why he couldn't take women there. Except that bank officials, like preachers, are supposed to be above reproach, and he did have neighbors. It struck me that he was being rather careless of his reputation, considering his position.

If I phrased it just right, I decided, I might be able to negotiate the maximum unsecured loan of a thousand dollars from my banker brother-in-law.

The next day, which was a Thursday, I dropped by the bank about two P.M. When I stuck my head in Arnold's office, he didn't exactly greet me with enthusiasm, but he wasn't unpleasant.

"Hello, Mel," he said. "Come on in." He pushed aside a letter he had been frowning over.

Closing his office door behind me, I took a chair in front of his desk and offered him a cigarette. When he merely shook his head, I lit one myself and dropped the match in his spotless desk ashtray.

"What's on your mind?" he asked.

I blew a stream of smoke in his direction. "I got to thinking we ought to patch up our grudge, Arnold. After all, we're brothers-in-law."

"I'm holding no grudge, Mel. I would never hire you again, and I have no intention of loaning you money, if that's what you're after. But I'm perfectly willing to be civil. I would even give you a job recommendation, providing the job didn't involve handling money."

I gave him a wounded look.

"Well, you could hardly expect me to recommend you to another bank," he said reasonably. "If you want any kind of recommendation, you're going to have to ask for it fast. Tomorrow's my last day here."

"You're retiring?" I asked in surprise.

"At forty-five? Hardly." He tossed me the letter he had been reading when I arrived.

The letterhead was of the Leveret branch of the Foster National Bank, and the letter read:

Dear Mr. Strong:

As per your last communication, we will expect you on the 2:10 P.M. train from Midway City on Monday, September 14th.

Unfortunately I will be unable to meet your train because of a prior commitment, so I am having our head bookkeeper, Miss Stella Marshall, meet you. I have reserved a room for you at the Leveret Hotel, and Miss Marshall will either drive you there or to the bank, as you prefer. I will be at the bank until five P.M., if you wish to see me Monday afternoon. Otherwise, I will look forward to meeting you Tuesday morning.

I am cordially looking forward to our acquaintanceship, and to a long and pleasant relationship as your assistant.

The letter was signed by Raymond Burke, Head Cashier.

"What's that all about?" I asked as I handed the letter back.

"I'm being transferred," he said in a doleful voice. "The Leveret branch manager died of a heart attack a few days ago, and they're sending me there to take over."

"You don't sound very happy about it."

"Well it's a promotion. I become full vice-president. But it's a strange community, and I've been happy here. I hate to leave all my friends."

Including Tina Crawford, I wondered. I said, "You must have some friends in the bank there."

He shook his head. "I knew old Sam Morrison, the former branch manager, but he's dead. This is a new branch, only activated about a month ago, and I've never met any of the employees. I don't know a soul in the town."

Out of nowhere a fantastic thought struck me. I said, "No one at all?"

"I've never been to Leveret. It's three hundred miles across the state, and I've never had occasion even to drive through it."

I suddenly forgot my plans to wrangle a loan as a fantastic thought took root in my mind. I asked, "How come you're going by train instead of driving?"

"My car's due for a trade-in, so I'm selling it and buying a new car when I get there. I've already sold the house and furniture. I was fortunate enough to find a buyer who wanted a furnished house. The new owner has a set of keys, so all I have to do Monday morning is walk out."

"What time does your train leave Monday?" I asked.

"At five-thirty in the morning. Why?"

"You've done me a few favors in the past. I'll pick you up and drive you to the station."

"Thanks, but I've already booked a taxi."

For what I had in mind, it wasn't really necessary for me to pick him up, so I let it drop. Punching out my cigarette, I rose and offered my hand.

"Well, good luck, Arnold. I'm glad I got to see you before you left."

Rising also, he gave me a cordial handshake. "Thanks, Mel. Good luck to you, too. That offer of a recommendation still stands."

"I don't need one," I told him. "I'm doing fine. I just dropped in to patch up our differences."

When I left the bank, I drove out to Riverview Point, parked and gazed out over the river while I thought. And gradually, as my plans crystalized, the thought which had struck me in Arnold's office became less and less fantastic and more and more workable.

Since Arnold knew no one in Leveret, it followed that no one there knew him. From my three years as a teller, I knew enough about banking procedure to fake my way through at least a couple of days. And that was all it would take.

A bank manager quite naturally has access to the vault, knows the combination, and even has keys to the building. If I had the guts to go through with it, I could walk off with a fortune and be out of the country before the theft was discovered.

The only trouble was, I couldn't see any possible way to work the plan without committing murder. I sat thinking until it began to get dark, without being able to solve the problem. I finally decided that big stakes were worth a big risk. I didn't particularly like Arnold, anyway.

As my first problem was to dispose of my brother-in-law in such a way that he wouldn't be missed, I concentrated on that. I realized the timing would have to depend on Arnold's weekend plans. It would be disastrous, for example, if the bank had scheduled a Saturday night going-away party for him, and the guest of honor failed to show up.

The simplest way to learn his plans was to ask him. At eight-thirty I phoned his home. When he answered, I said, "This is Mel, Arnold. I've been thinking that I owe you a lot for past favors, and I would like to give you a little send-off party by taking you out to dinner before you leave. Or are you all tied up with parties over the weekend?"

"No, the bank employees gave me a banquet last Saturday. I'm not going to be in town over the weekend, though."

"Oh? I thought you didn't leave until Monday."

"I don't, but I'm going fishing up at Bemus Lake. I sold the car a couple of hours ago, but the man agreed to let me keep it over the weekend, and he'll pick it up sometime Monday. I'm driving up to the lake tomorrow evening and won't be back until Sunday evening. I'm afraid I won't feel much like celebrating then, because I have to catch a five-thirty train Monday morning."

I made my voice rueful. "I guess that's out then. Who are you going fishing with?"

"No one. I'm driving up alone."

Things were working out beautifully. I said, "Well, good luck at the lake."

"Thanks," he said. "And thanks for your invitation, even though I can't take it."

After I hung up, I sat thinking until I had every detail of my plan worked out. Then I went to bed and got a good night's sleep.

Friday morning I did some shopping in a hardware store. I bought four window sash weights and a dozen feet of sash cord. I stored my purchases in the trunk of my car.

On the chance that Arnold might take off work early on his last day and louse up all my plans by starting for the lake before I got to him, I decided to keep him under observation. At 2 P.M. I parked in a lot across from the bank. Arnold's sedan was in the bank's parking lot.

At four-thirty, bookkeepers and tellers began to filter out. By five most of the employees had left. It was another ten minutes before Arnold and Norman Brady came out together.

They walked onto the parking lot, stood alongside Norman Brady's car talking for a few moments, then shook hands. Brady climbed into his car and Arnold walked on to his. I waited until both cars had driven away before leaving the parking lot.

At Arnold's house the garage door was open and the sedan was in the garage. It was a couple of minutes after I rang the side bell before he answered the door. He looked at me in surprise.

"I was upstairs finishing my packing," he said. "Sorry I kept you waiting. Come in."

I stepped inside and he closed the door behind me. He was still wearing his suit coat and a necktie, I noted. The first thing I did when I walked into my furnished room was get comfortable, but Arnold had always been a bit formal.

"Go ahead with what you were doing," I said. "I just dropped by to say good-bye."

"I was closing the last suitcase when you rang the bell. I'm all finished. I can't offer you a drink because I've cleaned everything except the furniture out of the house."

"That's all right," I said, walking slowly on into the front room.

Following, he examined me a bit dubiously.

"Anybody else in the house?" I asked. "Expecting anyone?"

He gave me a puzzled look. "No. I was planning to leave in a few minutes."

Smiling, I moved toward him. He was totally unprepared for the karate chop I smashed into the side of his neck with all the force I could muster.

With a grunt he fell to his knees, his expression grew blank, and he pitched forward onto his face.

A karate chop, forcefully enough administered, is supposed to be able to kill a man by breaking his neck. But Arnold must have had a tough neck, because he was still breathing when I rolled him over on his back. When I gave him another chop just above the bridge of his nose, I could feel the bone crush beneath the stiffened edge of my palm. Reflex action brought his knees up to his chest. Then his breathing stopped.

Rising, I went to check the front, back and side doors to make sure they were locked, then returned to the body. Rolling the dead man onto his side, I took the wallet from his hip pocket and examined it. It contained plenty of identification, in case I had to establish that I was Arnold Strong. The description on the driver's license didn't fit me, but nobody but a cop ever reads a driver's-license description when it is presented for identification. The wallet also contained something over two hundred dollars in bills.

I transferred my own wallet to my inner breast pocket and put Arnold's on my hip. In his coat pocket I found a set of car keys and a ring of other keys. The latter I tried on the side door until I found one that worked. I pocketed both sets.

Upstairs, in a bedroom I found two suitcases and a satchel, all packed. The briefcase I had seen Arnold carrying lay on the bed, and it occurred to me there might be some papers in it that the new branch manager of the Foster National Bank of Leveret ought to be familiar with. It was empty, however.

I made two trips to carry the luggage and the briefcase downstairs. Then, since there was no more I could do until after dark, and I didn't care to sit around for hours with a dead man, I let myself out the side door and locked it behind me.

I returned just before eleven P.M., backed my car into the driveway and parked by the side door. Getting the sash weights and cord from the trunk, I let myself indoors, then listened cautiously.

The house was pitch dark, but with the aid of a match I found a lamp and turned it on. Arnold lay just as I had left him.

Quickly I stripped the body. I hefted the two suitcases, decided the lighter one probably contained more room and opened it. I got his underclothing, shirt and trousers into it, but there simply wasn't room to cram in shoes and coat. As it was, I had to sit on it to get it closed.

I managed to squeeze the coat into the second suitcase, but it wouldn't take the shoes. I could tell by the feel of the satchel it was so full it wouldn't take a pair of shoes. Then I thought of the briefcase and my problem was solved.

I bound a sash weight to each arm and each leg of the nude body. Going out the side door, I opened the car trunk and glanced around. There were lights in the house next door, but it was a good fifty feet away and the glow from its windows didn't reach this far. The only light I had turned on was the front-room lamp, so no light spilled from the open side door.

I'm a fairly powerful man, but I was sweating when I got the body safely stowed in the trunk.

I had the luggage and briefcase in the back seat, had turned off the lamp and locked the side door when it occurred to me that Arnold might have packed fishing gear in the trunk of the sedan. The new owner of the car might think it odd, I thought, and there was no point in leaving any loose ends. I checked, but none was there.

Probably it was stored somewhere in the garage, I decided. I didn't want to risk turning on the garage light to look, so I let it go. I put the keys in the ignition of the car and closed the garage door.

There is seldom any traffic on the Riverview Point Bridge at midnight. When I parked in its center, there were no headlights in sight behind me and only a single pair approaching. I waited until they passed, then quickly got out of the car and opened the trunk.

I had just heaved the body over the rail when headlights turned onto the bridge a quarter mile behind me. Below, a dull splash almost coincided with my slamming of the trunk lid. I was raising the hood, as though I had motor trouble, when the car swooshed by. No other cars appeared while I was heaving over the luggage and the briefcase.

I was home and in bed by one A.M. Saturday morning I drove to a used car lot and sold my car. The rest of Saturday and all day Sunday I spent practicing Arnold's signature, as it appeared on his driver's license. This probably was an unnecessary precaution, I felt, but according to the letter Arnold had shown me, he had been in correspondence with the head cashier, and the man just might notice a difference in signature if I had to sign anything.

I didn't have much packing to do, since I lived in a furnished room and owned nothing but clothing. Sunday night I gave my landlady notice, and a taxi picked me up and my two suitcases at a quarter to five Monday morning.

On the train I had over eight hours to do nothing but worry, and I began to think of a hundred pitfalls in my plan. Suppose some bank employee was a former resident of Midway City who knew either me or Arnold Strong by sight? Suppose some member of the board of trustees decided to visit the Leveret branch? Even if a board member, or someone from the Midway City branch, merely phoned to talk to Arnold Strong, my masquerade would fail, because my voice didn't sound like Arnold's.

I think I would have abandoned the whole idea if I hadn't already taken the irrevocable step of murder. I was determined to get out of the country, and I didn't want to leave it as a pauper.

Finally, I managed to calm myself by deciding to spend as little time as possible at the bank. I would postpone my first visit there until Tuesday morning, and once I had the vault combination and the necessary keys, I would conveniently get sick and be confined to my hotel room until I was ready to move.

Stella Marshall, the head bookkeeper, turned out to be a prim, middle-aged spinster. She showed no surprise at my appearance, which was one hurdle over. I was six years younger than Arnold, and probably the new branch manager's age was known to at least the executive personnel, because it was only natural that there would have been some discussion about Arnold among them. Either it didn't occur to her, or she took me for a youthful forty-five.

I told her I was coming down with a cold and wasn't up to visiting the bank that day, so she drove me to the Leveret Hotel.

En route she said, "Mr. Burke didn't know your plans for permanent housing, so he hasn't done anything about lining up a house or apartment until you tell him your preference."

"How far is the bank from the hotel?" I asked.

"Only a block and a half."

"Then temporarily I would just as soon stay there. I have no family, you know."

"Yes," she said. "Mr. Burke told me you were a widower."

When she dropped me at the hotel, she offered to come by to pick me up the next morning, but since the bank was so close, I told her I preferred to walk.

The next morning I arrived at the bank promptly at nine A.M. Raymond Burke, the head cashier and the branch's second ranking officer, turned out to be a thin, balding man of about thirty-five, with thick-lensed glasses. He, like Stella Marshall, accepted me at face value.

I made a pretense of blowing my nose at about two-minute intervals and complained that I felt an attack of flu coming on. Burke seemed properly sympathetic.

After showing me my private office, he took me on a tour of the bank, introducing me to the personnel at the same time he showed me the facilities. When everyone greeted me with polite friendliness and complete lack of suspicion, I began to breathe easier.

We got to the vault last. It was identical to the one at Midway City, so I didn't have to have it explained to me.

"Mr. Morrison always set the time vault at five, with either me or Miss Marshall as a witness," Burke said. "Since his death, I've been setting it with her as a witness. Will you want to take over that responsibility?"

"Yes," I said. "Where's the register?"

He showed me the vault register, which was merely a large notebook. In it, each afternoon, the person who closed the vault entered the number of hours which had been set on the dial and initialed it. The witness also initialed the entry.

We returned to my private office and Burke indicated a thick manilla folder on my desk.

"That's a résumé of all the bank's activities, which I had drawn up for your convenience," he said. "You'll find all the assets and liabilities listed, a complete list of loans, investments and so forth. If you have any questions, just give a yell."

"Thanks," I said. "It will probably take me most of the day to go over everything, so I would just as soon not be disturbed. Suppose for today, at least, you carry on just as you have been before I arrived."

"Of course. I'll pass the word to leave you alone today."

When he went out and closed the door behind him, I opened the folder. Most of the contents were of no interest to me, but one item interested me considerably. Cash on hand, as of closing time the day before, was listed as $251,372.87.

A quarter of a million dollars, I thought. Of course a portion of that would consist of one-dollar bills and change, but even if fifty thousand of it was too bulky to carry off, two hundred thousand would remain. I wondered if the figure represented the average amount of cash left in the vault at night.

Except for a lunch break, I spent all day secluded in my office, actually going over the data, in case Raymond Burke wanted to discuss the bank's affairs.

Just before five I emerged and asked the head cashier if the vault were ready to be closed.

"Yes," he said. "I took the liberty of already setting the combination."

He handed me a slip of paper listing the numbers he had chosen. A new combination was set each night, and the numbers were written down on two slips. The person who set the time lock carried one, the witness the other.

"Incidentally, here are your keys to the building," he said, handing me two brass keys. "This is to the front door, this to the back." He indicated each with a pointing finger.

We went over to the vault together and he handed me the time-set key. I made sure the bolt was drawn, as setting the lock when it isn't jams the mechanism. Opening the glass door, I inserted the key in the hole below the first clock dial.

"We set it to open at nine-fifteen," Burke said. "That would be sixteen and a quarter hours."

I turned the key until sixteen and a quarter was indicated, withdrew the key, closed the glass door, shut the vault and twisted the handle which drove the bolt home.

Entering the time in the vault register, I initialed it *A.S.*

Raymond Burke placed his initials behind mine.

I had already decided that Friday night was the logical time to hit the vault, as that would give me until Monday morning before the theft was discovered. Meantime, the less time I spent at the bank, the less chance there was of my unmasking.

Wednesday morning I phoned the bank at nine-fifteen, made my voice hoarse and asked for Burke. When he answered, I said in the same hoarse voice, "This is Arnold Strong, Burke. I'm flat in bed with a case of flu. I hate to miss work on only my second day, but I just can't make it."

"Oh, I'm sorry," he said. "Anything I can do for you?"

"No. The doctor advises bed rest. He also advises no visitors. For their protection, not mine. I guess this stuff is pretty contagious. I can order anything I need from room service, so I'll be all right. I'll either be in tomorrow or phone you."

"All right, Mr. Strong," he said. "Don't worry about anything. We'll carry on."

As soon as he hung up, I phoned the airport and inquired about flights out of the country. There were no after-midnight flights leaving until six A.M. I reserved a space under my own name for six A.M. Saturday morning. That would put me out of reach before the empty vault was discovered. Then I went out, located a pawn shop and bought a leather valise.

Thursday morning I again phoned Burke and told him I was as ill as ever.

"Take all the time you need," he said. "We're getting along all right. Mr. Redding phoned yesterday, but he only wanted to see how you were getting on. When I told him you were ill, he asked that you call him when you return to work."

Byron Redding was chairman of the board of trustees of the central bank. If I had been there to receive the call, I would have been in the soup.

"I'll call him from here," I said. "I'm well enough to make a phone call."

Friday morning I phoned the bank again, this time without a hoarse voice. "I think I'm getting better," I said. "I'm still a little dizzy, but I'm going to try to make it this afternoon. Expect me before closing time."

"All right," Burke said. "It really isn't necessary to come down if you don't feel up to it, though."

"I'm sure I'll be up to it," I assured him.

I got to the bank just before three. Burke followed me into my office. I said, "Is there any water around here? It's time for my flu medicine."

"I'll get you some," he said, going back out. He returned carrying a paper cup of water.

"Thanks," I said, swallowing the pill and chasing it with water.

"Mr. Redding phoned again this morning," he said. "Also a Mr. Brady from Midway City called you about an hour ago. I told both you would be in before three, and would call back."

I was wondering how I was going to get out of making the calls when he pointed to the two phones on my desk.

"That phone on the left goes through the switchboard," he said. "The other is a direct line outside."

"Fine," I said. "Now if you'll excuse me, I'd better make the call-backs."

He went out and closed the door behind him.

I didn't make either phone call, of course, but there was no way for Burke to know that. I sat there sweating out the passage of time, hoping neither man would decide to call again.

When my watch said five to five and the phone had not yet rung, I got up and left my office. Burke came from the direction of the vault at the same time, and we met in the middle of the room.

"The combination is already set," he said, handing me the slip of paper containing it and the time-clock key.

Putting the paper in my pocket, I moved toward the vault with Burke at my side. At the wooden gate which gave entry to the vault area I paused, took out my pill bottle and shook a tablet into my hand.

"I'm due for another one of these," I said. "Would you mind getting me some water again?"

"Of course not," he said, starting for the water fountain across the room.

Pushing through the gate, I checked the vault bolt and opened the glass door. I set the clock for seven hours, removed the key, closed the glass door and swung the vault door shut. I had just driven home the bolt when Burke returned with the cup of water.

He looked a trifle surprised that the vault was already locked, but he didn't say anything. I accepted the water, took my pill and tossed the empty cup into a nearby waste basket.

In the vault register I entered that the time lock had been set for sixty-four and a quarter hours. I initialed the entry and Burke put his intials behind mine.

"Good night," I said pleasantly. "See you Monday morning."

There was no one on the street when I returned at midnight. I carried my valise up the alley behind the bank and let myself in the rear door.

Fifteen minutes later I let myself out again, the valise now crammed with every bill of five dollars or more which had been in the vault. I hadn't stopped to count it, but I estimated it was in excess of two hundred thousand dollars.

When I got back to the hotel, I left a call for four-thirty A.M., and asked that a cab be ready to take me to the airport at five-fifteen.

It took me until one in the morning to count the money. It came to slightly over two hundred and three thousand dollars. I had just relatched the valise when a knock came at the door. Tossing the valise into the closet, I went over and opened the door. Two strange men stood there.

The taller said, "Mr. Arnold Strong?"

"Yes," I said.

Showing a badge, he moved into the room, his stockier companion following.

"What is this?" I asked.

"What made you think you could get away with it, Mr.

Strong?" the tall man inquired. "The initial hundred-thousand-dollar shortage might have taken some time to uncover, because you rigged it pretty cleverly. As a matter of fact, the head bookkeeper says it might have gone undiscovered for months if this last shortage hadn't started him digging. You must have known this second hundred grand you walked off with would be discovered in a matter of days, even with that forged promissory note you planted in the files. Why didn't you head south?"

As I stared at him in numb shock, it penetrated that I wasn't the only embezzler connected with Foster National Bank. No wonder Arnold had been less than enthusiastic about the transfer. The night I saw him at the Thirty-three Club must not have been his first visit there, if he had been covering up a hundred-grand shortage at the bank.

Then it registered on me that one cop was implying Arnold had walked off with a second hundred thousand in cash. I thought of the briefcase I had seen him carry from the bank, later lying empty on his bed.

He hadn't been planning a weekend fishing trip, I realized. He had been planning to drive to the airport, abandon his car and skip the country.

Why hadn't I searched his luggage, I wondered sickly? I had tossed a hundred thousand dollars into the river.

In a dull tone I said, "I'm not really Arnold Strong. I'm his brother-in-law, Melvin Hall."

"Yeah?" the tall man said, producing handcuffs. "Where's Strong then?"

That was going to take a lot of explaining, I thought, as the handcuffs snapped into place.

CONTENTS: ONE BODY

by C. B. Gilford

WHEN MRS. KERLEY had her scene with Anita Lowe that Monday afternoon, she didn't know, of course, that it would be the last one. There would be no more scenes because she would never see Anita Lowe again.

But this last scene was worthy of the combatants. The other tenants had wondered for a while why Mrs. Kerley had allowed Anita Lowe to stay on in 2-A. But they finally understood why. Mrs. Kerley was a belligerent sort, happiest when she had the most to complain about, when she had someone to bawl and shout at. Mr. Kerley had served in that capacity until he wearied of it and died. After him came a succession of tenants, the present incumbent Anita Lowe. And why should Anita Lowe have endured Mrs. Kerley? Because Mrs. Kerley allowed goings-on that other landladies wouldn't have. She allowed them, of course, so she could complain about them. A curious but satisfactory arrangement, all in all.

On that last afternoon—as far as anyone knows the last afternoon of Anita Lowe's life—the tenants in 1-B and 2-B heard at least portions of the scene. They may even have heard the beginning of it, which was Anita's knock on Mrs. Kerley's door.

Mrs. Kerley was sitting in her front window, her favorite observation post. The high-school girl across the street was dawdling with a male youngster in tight blue jeans and leather jacket, and Mrs. Kerley was clucking in disapproval. The knock at the door was an interruption, and Mrs. Kerley went to answer the summons in a hostile mood.

Although it was four o'clock in the afternoon, Anita Lowe was standing there in a flimsy housecoat beneath which was an even flimsier nightgown. And she was barefooted.

Mrs. Kerley decided to smile. "Come in, dearie," she said. "You'll catch your death of cold out there in the hall." Sometimes she liked to invite people into her apartment, so that she could have the possible pleasure later of ordering them out.

But Anita, despite her knowledge of her landlady's character, accepted the invitation. She came in and sat tiredly on the sofa. Ordinarily quite pretty, almost beautiful, she was not at her best on this afternoon. She had made an attempt with a comb at her short blonde hair, she had dabbed at her mouth with lipstick, but no quick treatment could improve the slightly bloodshot condition of her eyes or the puffiness of her features. She looked as if she needed sleep badly, and maybe half a dozen aspirin.

"Now what's the trouble, my little fine-feathered friend?"

"Mrs. Kerley, I've just got to have a cup of coffee, and I forgot to get any when I was at the store yesterday."

Now why didn't Anita Lowe apply at 1-B or 2-B for a coffee loan? Mrs. Kerley knew the answer. Anita had done just that very thing dozens of times, had never remembered to return the borrowed property, and so had run out of credit. Whereas here at her place, due to their peculiar relationship, Anita might have to accept a piece of Mrs. Kerley's mind, but stood a chance of getting the coffee along with it.

"Instant, if you have any," Anita added.

A mood of diabolical generosity was upon Mrs. Kerley. "I'll go you one better than that," she said. "I'll fix you a cup right here."

Anita tried to protest, but her hostess was not to be denied. Mrs. Kerley exited to the kitchen, leaving Anita fumbling vainly in her pocket for a cigarette. That was luxury Mrs. Kerley didn't furnish. But she did have the instant variety of coffee. The water boiled quickly. Mrs. Kerley brought down two cups and two saucers from her good china, spooned coffee, poured the steaming liquid over it, and returned to the living room in swift triumph.

Anita needed the refreshment too much to brood over the curious fact of having an afternoon tête-à-tête with her landlady. She sipped desperately at the coffee, ignoring its temperature.

"You needed a little pick-up, is that it?" Mrs. Kerley asked.

The blonde girl didn't even bother to nod.

"Must have had quite a late night, eh?"

That jolted Anita to attention. She knew Mrs. Kerley's opinion of late nights. "Oh, I didn't just get up, if that's what you mean," she said quickly. "I was up early. But then I got this awful headache, so I lay down for a nap. And I woke up with a worse headache than ever."

Mrs. Kerley smiled with sweet understanding. "It figures," she said.

Anita Lowe suffered from a psychosis which demanded that she conceal her guilt with loud protests of innocence. "If you mean," she answered haughtily, "that you think I had something to drink last night, you're very wrong."

But Mrs. Kerley, enjoying herself immensely, was off in a slightly different direction. "Arthur . . . Mr. Lowe . . . is on quite an extended trip this time, isn't he? Been gone for how long now?"

"Two weeks," Anita answered.

"Gets lonesome, doesn't it?"

Anita had been accused before, but she'd never gotten used to it. "Sure it gets lonesome," she answered hotly. "I'm so crazy about Arthur . . ."

At that Mrs. Kerley threw back her head and laughed derisively.

"If Arthur only had a job where he didn't have to travel . . ."

Mrs. Kerley laughed again.

"Shut up, you old hag!"

Such a frank expression of opinion from a guest was surprise enough to Mrs. Kerley. But what happened next was even more surprising, and more painful. There was half a cup of still hot coffee in Anita Lowe's hand. In the next instant, the coffee left the cup, sailed through the air, and splashed on Mrs. Kerley, some of it on her face, the rest down the front of her dress not quite scalding, but decidedly warm.

For a few seconds Mrs. Kerley was immobilized by shock. Long enough for Anita to dash the good china cup and saucer to the floor, to stride to the door, open it, and disappear into the hallway. When Mrs. Kerley herself finally leaped up and managed the door, all she saw of Anita was a wisp of nightgown disappearing around the turn of the stairs.

Frustrated in her pursuit, Mrs. Kerley could only bellow. "Get out of my apartment, you hussy! You can pack up and leave right now, you trollop!" She screamed other names also, more colorful and more explicit.

Anita, of course, slammed and bolted the door of 2-A and didn't return to the fray. Mrs. Pearson, however, came down from 2-B, and Mrs. Schwartz peeked out from 1-B and were treated to a sight of Mrs. Kerley's coffee-drenched face and bosom and an account of the battle.

"Did you see what she did to me?" Mrs. Kerley wailed.

Mrs. Pearson and Mrs. Schwartz saw and sympathized.

"And broke a nice cup and saucer of mine too."

"The one with the rose buds?" Mrs. Pearson asked in horror.

"With the rose buds. She'll pay for this!"

Mrs. Schwartz ducked back inside 1-B as soon as she could. Mrs. Pearson edged slowly up the stairs and escaped at the next opportunity. Mrs. Kerley was left alone again in the lower hallway, still hurling imprecations upward for another full ten minutes, taunting her enemy to come back down again. Gradually then, by slow stages, as the formidable dame slowly succumbed to exhaustion, the building quieted down.

Mrs. Kerley brooded the rest of that afternoon. That brooding was important because it kept her wakeful. She saw a little bit with her cat's eyes that functioned rather well even in the dark. But she heard a lot more with ears that were attuned to the significant squeaking of floor-boards.

It was eight-thirty and after dark, for instance, when the car appeared across the street, lights off, waiting. It could have been the blue-jeans boy after the high-school girl, but it wasn't. It wasn't that sort of car.

Within seconds of Mrs. Kerley's spotting the car, there were meaningful sounds from upstairs in 2-A. Sharp, staccato cracklings on the floor. Anita Lowe's spike heels. Then the hallway door of 2-A stealthily opening and closing.

Mrs. Kerley had a decision to make then. Whether or not to intercept Anita at the foot of the stairs, expose her infidelity to the neighborhood in loud tones, and demand immediate evacuation of her premises. But then supposing that the new tenant would turn out to be an innocent, shy, uninteresting little creature, someone impossible to find fault with? Still, there was that cup-of-coffee incident . . .

While Mrs. Kerley thus vacillated, Anita Lowe slipped down the stairs, out through the front door, down the walk, and across the street to the waiting car. The dome light flashed on momentarily while Anita's red-clad torso wriggled inside. There was a man at the wheel, of course.

"That hussy!" Mrs. Kerley spat out bitterly.

The night wore on. 1-B and 2-B were quiet. The Pearsons and the Schwartzes never went out. Overhead, 2-A was empty. The forsaken wife was being consoled elsewhere. Mrs. Kerley found sleep, even catnapping, impossible.

Then very suddenly, a new, unexpected sound brought Mrs. Kerley to a fully erect position in her rocking chair. Someone was inside the lower hall and on the stairs. Anita and her boy friend. No, there was only one person. Anita by herself. No, the step seemed different.

Up the stairs, and in the hallway above. A key grating in the lock of 2-A. The door opening and closing. Footsteps. A man's. Heavier and no spike heels. But no sound of a light switch clicking. Whoever it was, was moving around 2-A in the dark.

A burglar, Mrs. Kerley thought, gripping the chair arms in terror. But she calmed quickly. The man had had a key, so he couldn't be a burglar. And he was walking around confidently up there in the dark. It had to be Arthur Lowe.

But why in the dark?

Mrs. Kerley didn't know why, but the puzzle of it kept her listening with intense concentration. Arthur Lowe went into every room up there in 2-A. Looking for his wife obviously. And failing to find her, of course. Finally sitting down on the sofa, Mrs. Kerley heard the squeak of springs and the squish of cushions.

Arthur Lowe was sitting up there, waiting for his wife to come home. And he was sitting in the dark!

Mrs. Kerley was becoming excited now. Judging entirely by the sounds she could guess at the situation. Arthur Lowe had returned secretly, since Anita hadn't been expecting him. But he'd also returned stealthily. He hadn't expected to find his wife at home, but he'd searched to make sure. And now he was waiting for her, but he didn't want to warn her that he was waiting. Hence no lights.

Gloating, Mrs. Kerley could picture him up there on the sofa. Arthur Lowe, meek and mild-mannered, not too tall, slope-shouldered and perhaps a bit thin. His blue eyes peering from behind their spectacles unseeing into the darkness. What was the expression in those eyes, on his pale face?

Poor Arthur Lowe. He worked hard and made good money. But to make the money he had to travel. So he could afford to support Anita, but he could seldom be home to enjoy her company. What he'd really been doing all this time then was supporting her for the benefit of other men. And now—well, he'd either discovered that fact suddenly, or having realized it all along, he'd finally decided to do something about it.

What was that something going to be? Mrs. Kerley trembled with anticipation. She wasn't going to be there to see it happen, but hearing and imagining it would be the next best thing.

The night was a long one. Mrs. Kerley watched the illuminated hands of her alarm clock go around and around. From above, Arthur Lowe gave no indication that he was even alive. The sofa hadn't squeaked once since he'd first sat down on it. He was a patient man all right. But now apparently his patience was at an end.

It was three-thirty—Mrs. Kerley marked the time—when the car returned with Anita in it. Even at that late hour, however, it didn't disgorge its passenger right away. Mrs. Kerley grew almost frantic as the minutes slowly passed. It was almost four when the car door finally opened, the dome light flashed, and Anita in her red dress squirmed out. No, the man didn't attempt to come in with her. Anita knew what Mrs. Kerley would do if he tried that—she'd call the police.

The front door opened, a little noisily, a little clumsily. Anita probably thought her landlady was asleep. Up the stairs, a little wobbly on the spike heels. Fumbling with the key, finally getting the door open. No clicking of a light switch this time either. Anita was probably finding the darkness easier on her eyes.

Then it came. A man's voice, low and soft. Just a word or two. A little scream of surprise from Anita, hushed, muffled, not loud enough to wake anybody in any of the other apartments. A few seconds of silence, then a jumble of voices, husband and wife talking at the same time. But still, each for his or her own reason, quietly enough to avoid arousing the neighbors.

What were they saying to each other? What were Arthur's accusations, and how did Anita try to defend herself? Surely he didn't believe her for one moment. Mrs. Kerley strained to hear some words, but failed. She wished she had secret microphones set up in all the apartments, so she could listen in on all her tenants' conversations.

It went on how long? Maybe five minutes. Then the sofa squeaked. Arthur Lowe had risen to his feet. The noise level of the voices rose a little too, changed pitch a little, became shriller. It was mostly Anita's voice now. Could Mrs. Kerley be sure? Did Anita sound afraid? Was she finally realizing that Arthur meant business?

Silence. It happened so quickly that at first Mrs. Kerley thought she had lost her hearing. The argument upstairs had ended like a television play cut off by a blown picture tube. Action one moment, absolutely nothing the next.

Bursting with curiosity, Mrs. Kerley almost started to run upstairs to look for the cause of the sudden stillness. Surely they weren't in each other's arms, kissing! Surely Arthur had more gumption and spunk than that . . .

No, there were sounds again. Couldn't follow their significance. A sofa squeak. But not made by Arthur, because Arthur's footsteps began wandering around the apartment. Almost aimlessly, it seemed. Mrs. Kerley could detect no pattern in the movements. One light switch clicked finally. On, then right off again. Darkness. Arthur Lowe was pacing around in complete darkness. While Anita sat on the sofa.

No . . . the sofa was squeaking again. Then something going across the floor that wasn't footsteps. Was something being dragged? A piece of furniture? Living room to bedroom, and stopping there. Another squeak, unidentifiable. A thump. Squeaks again. Clicks.

Back to the sofa. Arthur's footsteps. Sitting down. Silence. Getting up again. More pacing. Just Arthur though. Anita had neither moved nor spoken for a long while now. It was nearly five o'clock, close to dawn.

Finally, just when Mrs. Kerley thought it never would, the pacing ceased. Arthur was at the door. Opening and shutting it. The click of the automatic lock. Arthur's footsteps coming down the stairs. Out the front door. From the window Mrs. Kerley watched him. He must have parked his car a distance away, perhaps to conceal his presence, because now he merely walked down the sidewalk and disappeared.

Well! That was strange, wasn't it? Arthur had come and gone, but what had he accomplished? Mrs. Kerley had been hoping to hear the sounds of blows, then of Anita's cries of pain. But there'd been nothing.

Mrs. Kerley didn't sleep. She listened for Anita, but didn't hear her. Mrs. Kerley was confused now. Anita definitely wasn't in bed. But was she on the sofa? Dawn came without that question being answered.

It was a miserable day for Mrs. Kerley. About noon, when she had the chance of doing it unobserved, she went upstairs and knocked at the door of 2-A. No result. After that, rather than climb the stairs again, she phoned. She could hear the bell ring up in 2-A. And ring and ring.

Anita Lowe had not left the apartment. Of that Mrs. Kerley could be certain. Arthur had departed alone. But long hours had passed now, and no sign of Anita.

With the coming of darkness again, Mrs. Kerley succumbed to exhaustion. But she slept only lightly, her ears tuned to possible noise from 2-A. When she woke in the morning, she was as certain as if she'd never slept at all, that 2-A had continued quiet as a tomb.

That was the morning when the long-distance telephone call came. Arthur Lowe was on the other end of the wire. His voice was mild, calm, matter-of-fact. "Mrs. Kerley? This is Arthur Lowe."

"Yes, Mr. Lowe." Mrs. Kerley tried to keep from sounding excited.

"Mrs. Kerley, my wife has just joined me here and has decided to stay with me for a while. We'll keep the apartment, of course. I'll mail the rent. But there are some things my wife would like to have, and they're all in that fancy trunk of hers upstairs. You know, the one with the flowers painted on it. Well, would you do us a favor? Call the express man, let him into our apartment, have him pick up the trunk, and ship it to us collect."

He rattled off the precise address then, and in a daze Mrs. Kerley wrote it down. Automatically, because Arthur Lowe was so insistent, she promised to do as he requested. Then he hung up.

Mrs. Kerley dashed up the stairs a pair at a stride. Her duplicate key opened the door of 2-A quickly. Inside, her eye made a hasty inspection. There was nothing disturbed or awry.

She walked from the living room into the bedroom. There at the foot of the double bed was the trunk. Not a large one, maybe three or three and a half feet long, less than two wide and maybe two deep. It was painted green with an overlay of red roses. There was no need for Mrs. Kerley even to touch the thing to realize that it was securely locked.

She knew the whereabouts of Anita Lowe then.

The murder had occurred on Monday night. Or more precisely, a bit before dawn on Tuesday morning. On Wednesday morning Arthur Lowe had phoned long-distance. It was on the following Monday that the special-delivery letter came, urgently repeating the request for the trunk, and pleading, if it had already been shipped, for Mrs. Kerley to check on its progress. As she had with the phone call, Mrs. Kerley ignored it.

She had made up her mind on the subject. She wasn't mourning the death of Anita Lowe. In fact, she rejoiced in it. Only justice had been done. Consequently she had no desire to turn Arthur Lowe over to the police.

But there was herself to consider. She had suffered a great deal at Anita's hands. The incident of the coffee had been merely the last, not the first. Things like that demanded justice, too. Payment. And now that Arthur Lowe didn't have Anita's present demands to meet, he could well afford to settle her past debts. Mrs. Kerley hadn't decided on the exact amount. But she knew she could collect it. Because she had possession of the trunk.

Mrs. Kerley had begun to enjoy the sense of power that trunk gave her. If a psychologist had gotten hold of Mrs. Kerley, he might ultimately have concluded that this thirst for power was the real reason why Mrs. Kerley enjoyed being a landlady. It allowed her to control the roof over people's heads, to make rules, to enforce those rules. So even though she had her eye on turning a profit eventually, at the moment Mrs. Kerley enjoyed her blackmail scheme for its own sake.

Come to think of it, she didn't care much more for Arthur Lowe than she had for his wife. Hadn't he been the one who'd complained about the lack of janitor service?

Justice, that was all that Mrs. Kerley wanted. Justice.

Airily she consigned Arthur Lowe's special delivery to the wastebasket, and sat down to pen him a teasing little note:

Dear Mr. Lowe:

In answer to your letter concerning your wife, I feel that I am able to put your mind at ease. Don't worry about Mrs. Lowe for one minute. She is in good hands. You can trust me completely. I'll keep an eye on her for you. She isn't able to write to you at the moment, which is why I'm writing instead. But I thought you might be interested to know. Your wife doesn't go out any more at all. She seems quite satisfied to stay at home. So don't worry.

Sincerely, Emma Kerley.

That would bring him running, she thought. Make him sweat too. Make him realize that Emma Kerley was no amateur in little intrigues like this. She was a clever woman, so there was no use in his trying to figure out ways of getting around her.

Arthur Lowe arrived back in town within twenty-four hours. He didn't come by daylight. She hadn't expected him to. He came under cover of darkness, after midnight.

She heard him come through the front door, recognized his tread on the stairs. She heard him try his key, and afterwards test the stoutness of the door. Finally he descended the stairs again, knocked at her door.

"Come in, Mr. Lowe," she called.

He entered quickly, shut the door behind him in haste. Then he stood there staring at her, his thick spectacles enlarging his eyes till he looked rather like a thin, pale frog. He was a calm customer, but Mrs. Kerley had expected that, what with the quiet, efficient way he had murdered Anita, then walked off leaving her body in the trunk and trusting his landlady and a truck driver to get rid of it for him.

"The lock's been changed on the door of my apartment," he said.

Mrs. Kerley nodded.

"Why?"

"To protect the contents."

"I suppose you're the only one who has the key."

Mrs. Kerley nodded again.

"I should have known." He licked his lips. There was a film of sweat over his face, which accentuated the frog look. "Well then, shall we be frank with each other, Mrs. Kerley?"

She didn't really know Arthur Lowe very well, had never had much contact with him. She found herself wondering again just how he had killed Anita. She had decided on strangling, since there'd been no noise, and no sign of blood anywhere. She glanced at his hands now. They were small, pale. Of course he'd been very angry at Anita.

"That was a cleverly worded letter, Mrs. Kerley. But it omitted one important point. You've seized my property. What is your price for returning it?"

She rocked slowly in her rocking chair. "I'm not a greedy woman," she told him. "I merely want to be repaid for the mistreatment and the insults I got from your wife. I was patient with her for a long time, Mr. Lowe. I protected your good name. And I want to go on protecting your good name, Mr. Lowe. But I just want something for my trouble, that's all."

"How much?"

"We don't have to haggle. Some nice, round, convenient figure. Say ten thousand dollars."

He almost smiled, it seemed. She wasn't quite sure. "I don't have anywhere near that much money," he said.

"You could get it."

"I don't know how."

"I'll give you a little time. Your wife is being well taken care of meanwhile, as I said in my letter."

"Yes, your letter . . ."

"Don't get the idea you can break down that door in the middle of the night, Mr. Lowe. I'm a very light sleeper. I would simply call the police."

"Yes, the police . . ."

"But don't delay too long, Mr. Lowe." She was a little peeved that he wasn't cowering before her. "Your wife . . . your property . . . is still occupying my apartment. Starting tomorrow, the rent is a thousand dollars a day. Besides the ten thousand, that is."

His enormous eyes were expressionless. "I could always let you foreclose," he said.

"Then I would lose," she admitted. "But you wouldn't gain. Because the law would collect."

There didn't seem to be anything more to talk about after that. Arthur Lowe's frog stare was an uncomfortable thing to have to look back at, but Mrs. Kerley forced herself to do it.

"I'll be waiting right here whenever you have the money," she told him.

He didn't bother to say good-bye. He slipped out through the door quietly. She switched off the lamp, so she could watch him as he left the building. His car was nowhere in sight. He merely walked away, as he'd done the night he'd murdered Anita.

It was then, for the first time, that Mrs. Kerley shivered. For the first time her nerve began to crack. She almost threw open the window and shouted for him to come back and take that green trunk. She wanted to call the police and report her "suspicion."

But the weakness passed quickly. Yes, she was dealing with a murderer. Not a hardened murderer though. And Arthur Lowe couldn't dispose of her as easily as he'd disposed of his wife. Granted, he might feel like killing her. But as Arthur Lowe had already discovered, murder is a complicated business. His first murder he'd planned to conceal by shipping the body off in a trunk. But what would he do with a second body?

Surely it couldn't be squeezed into the same trunk!

The thought seized Mrs. Kerley like a python attacking its prey. It wrapped its slimy coils around her, opened its jaws and tried to swallow her. She fought back, in panic at first, then gradually with some small logic.

Wasn't Arthur Lowe's whole problem the disposal of corpses? And he only had one trunk. One can't carry a body around in a hatbox or a suitcase. Mrs. Kerley reflected, receiving some comfort from it, that she was no small woman. She was a good fifty pounds heavier than Anita had been, and bulkier in proportion. It was impossible to fit two bodies into that trunk. Wasn't it? Well, the thing to do was to take another look at that trunk and see.

Once the resolve was made she acted quickly upon it. She went to the silver vase where the key to the new lock was hidden, and fished it out. Then a flashlight. She didn't want to turn the lights on upstairs. It wouldn't do to attract Arthur Lowe's attention if he were still hanging around.

She ascended the stairs silently, having learned long ago how to move with stealth. The new key made a slight noise in the new lock, but it worked easily. The door was much worse. The squeak of its hinges was loud and raucous in Mrs. Kerley's ears, making her realize suddenly and for the first time why it had always been so easy for her to keep track of Anita's comings and goings.

Well, the only thing to do then to avoid more of that squeaking than absolutely necessary was to keep the door ajar. She'd only be a moment. She merely wanted another close look at that trunk, to measure it with her eyes, get a better idea of its capacity.

She entered the living room, the flashing beam probing ahead of her. Quick to the bedroom. Yes, the trunk was still there.

It was an ugly thing really. The green was of a ghastly shade, and the roses garish and too red. Or perhaps it only seemed so, because Mrs. Kerley knew that the trunk was actually a coffin and the colors were not befitting a coffin.

Never mind that though. Her mind was wandering. What about the size? Three and a half feet long, wasn't it? Or maybe four? Why hadn't she remembered to bring along her measuring tape? Length didn't matter though. A body could be doubled up. Two of them? How deep was the trunk? Two feet anyway. Now if you intertwined the arms and legs . . . with her knees in Anita's face, and Anita's knees . . .

It could be done!

The terror struck at Mrs. Kerley then. She wanted to scream, and actually tried to, but managed only a dry croak. Why was she afraid? Of the trunk? No, more than that. The squeaking! Yes, squeaking. The hallway door was being pushed farther open. She was trapped! He was here! Trapped!

She heard footsteps now, soft across the living room rug. What a fool she'd been. She'd let him in, made it easy for him. Why, he wouldn't even have to drag her body to the trunk. She was standing right beside it. And this time there'd be no witness downstairs to eavesdrop on the sounds of murder.

She was going to be murdered! Would he bury the trunk? She and Anita Lowe together in the same grave! Why couldn't she scream? Mrs. Pearson . . . Mrs. Schwartz . . . somebody . . .

Suddenly it was no longer dark. She heard the click first, and then the ceiling light flooded on. She whirled to face her murderer.

But Arthur Lowe wasn't alone. Two men were behind him, two men who looked somehow like detectives. And Arthur Lowe was the one who was screaming.

"Officers, look in that trunk! See if she put my wife in there . . ."

The circumstantial evidence all pointed in the wrong direction. The doctors set the date of death rather accurately, and Arthur Lowe was out of town at that time, and nobody could prove otherwise. If there'd been a long-distance phone call, as Mrs. Kerley claimed, it must have been from a pay booth, so there was no record of it. As for the letter, she'd thrown that away.

On the other hand, Mrs. Pearson and Mrs. Schwartz seemed to take a certain satisfaction in describing the trouble between Mrs. Kerley and Anita Lowe on the very day the doctors said Anita Lowe had died. And they hadn't seen Anita since either. They could picture it, all right. Mrs. Kerley had always been a little crazy, and she'd had a violent temper.

The worst thing, of course, was the letter which Arthur Lowe had thoughtfully waved. After all. "Your wife doesn't go out any more at all," and such. Who would know things like that except the person who'd murdered Anita Lowe?

THE TROUBLE WITH RUTH

by Henry Slesar

THE SOUND of the apartment door closing behind Ralph had an abruptness that struck Ruth like a blow.

The wall was growing between them; they both hated it and could do nothing about it. They'd been married almost ten years, and by unspoken agreement had never slept or said good-bye on an argument. But their lips were cold as Ralph had kissed her good-bye.

Ruth sighed and went into the living room. There was an opened pack of cigarettes on the television set. She lit one. It tasted black and horrible; she stamped it out. She went into the kitchen, poured herself a second cup of coffee, and sat down to wait. She knew just what to expect. In half an hour, her husband would arrive at his office. Five minutes later, he would be on the telephone tactlessly informing her mother about yesterday's episode, the third in three weeks. Her mother's voice would be marvelously steady as she replied to him, but by the time she dialed Ruth's number the sobs would begin in her throat and the first words she uttered would emerge choked and grieving.

At a quarter of ten, the telephone rang.

Ruth picked it up, almost smiling at the accuracy of her prognostication. "Hello?"

It was her mother, of course, and the thin voice was gulping out words of sorrow and commiseration.

"Mama, please!" Ruth shut her eyes. "You'll just have to get used to the idea I steal, Mom. I can't help myself. Try to understand that—"

There was talk of doctors, and trips out of the country; things that Ruth said she and her husband could not afford.

"I know it's a sickness," she said. "I know it's not nice. It's better to be a murderer or an alcoholic nowadays. You get more sympathy . . ."

Her mother was crying.

"Please, Mama. You're not helping. You're not helping me this way at all."

When she found a silence long enough to say good-bye and hang up, Ruth returned to the living room, and put her head against the arm of the sofa.

The questions troubled her again. How does it happen? Why does such a thing begin? Why do I steal? Could a doctor—one of *those* doctors—help her? She shuddered. She had been a perfectly normal child. Her family had money, *some* money, anyway. They had lived in a fine two-story house overlooking San Francisco Bay. And she had been bright in school, a top-of-the-class student. Nobody brought home a longer row of A's on their report card, not even the two cool, distant young ladies who were Ruth's older sisters. Also, she was popular.

But she had stolen, even then. Her first crime—Fanny Ritter's pencil box, a beautiful thing of blue binding and secret compartments. She had made the mistake of displaying her new possession at home, and then they knew. *Everybody* knew. She was a thief!

Ruth Moody, now twenty-eight, sobbed in her living room for the troubles of a thirteen-year-old girl.

No, Ruth decided at last, as she had decided before. It couldn't be something in the past. Her past was good and innocent.

But the question remained unanswered: Why did she steal? Why did she take the spools of thread from the department store on Washington Avenue? The cheap pearl buttons from the notions counter? Why did she leave the dress shop on Fourth Avenue with an unpurchased evening bag?

They had understood. All of them. They had called Ralph. They realized she was not a shoplifter really, but a woman with a problem. Everything was handled very simply. Ralph paid for the merchandise taken, a proper bill of sale was tendered. Her name and her description recorded in the files for handy reference if ever it happened again . . .

At eleven o'clock, a ringing sound roused her. She had fallen asleep and first looked toward the telephone; then realized it was the doorbell.

The man in the doorway took off his hat when she appeared, but that was his only courteous gesture. He stepped inside without invitation, closing the door behind him. He was short and his face had the hot, quick-burned look of sunlamp treatments. His thick hair was glossy, and his clothes had too many sharp corners.

"You Ruth Moody?" he said.

"Yes." She was more annoyed than frightened.

He smiled, uncovering tobacco-stained teeth. "I got a little business to talk over, Mrs. Moody."

He nodded towards the living room. "Can we go inside?"

"What kind of business? If you're selling something—"

"I'm buying, Mrs. Moody." He chuckled. "All right if I sit down?" He was already sitting down, on the sofa, lifting his trousers at the knees to preserve the knife-edge crease. "I think you better listen," he said carefully. "It's about your husband."

Her hand clutched at her houserobe, and she took a seat across the width of the room.

"What do you mean?"

"I know something about your husband," he said. "And I know a lot more about you. Put them together—they can spell trouble." He laid his hat down on the cushion beside him.

"Mrs. Moody," he continued, "how would you like to make a thousand dollars?"

"What?" Ruth asked, puzzled.

"You heard right. I got a little proposition for you. If you go along, you'll get a thousand bucks in the mail. If you don't—well, your husband might have a hard time making ends meet. You get what I mean?"

"No!"

"Let me put it this way. If you were a man's boss, and you found out that the man's wife was a shoplifter—"

Ruth's hands flew to her mouth.

"There. You see what I mean? It makes a difference, don't it? I mean, these days a man's family is important in his work. Gotta think of the firm's reputation, and all that. You see what I mean, don't you?"

"How did you know?" Ruth said miserably. "Who told you that?"

"Don't ask me that, Mrs. Moody. Let's just say I got sources. But don't get upset. It's a sickness, you know, like pneumonia, or hay fever. You can't help yourself—"

Ruth looked at the man hard. Then she said: "How much do you want?"

He waved his hand. "I don't want your nickels and dimes, Mrs. Moody. Didn't I tell you? I'm here to *buy.*"

"Buy what?"

"Your services. All you got to do is play along with us, and you can have a thousand bucks. Take my word for it, you got nothing to lose."

"What do you want me to do?" Ruth said.

"I can't spell it out for you. But I got a friend, see? He'll tell you the details. All you gotta do now is put on your hat and coat and come with me. My friend'll outline the whole deal. It's real easy, believe me. You won't regret it for a minute—"

She stood up. "I'm not coming with you!"

"Suit yourself." He seemed genuinely unconcerned. "We're not desperate for your help, Mrs. Moody. But we thought we'd give you a break." He sighed, got up and took his hat off the sofa. "But if you don't want to play along—"

"You don't really mean this."

He smiled, reached into an inner pocket and withdrew a small business card. He read a penciled notation.

"Otto Mavius and Company, 420 Fifth Avenue. That's where your husband works, right?"

"But I'm not dressed!" she said frantically. "I can't come with you now!"

"I can wait, Mrs. Moody. I'm in no hurry."

They looked at each other for a while; then Ruth whirled and ran toward the bedroom.

In half an hour, they were in a taxi, and the man with the sunburn was giving the name of a modest downtown hotel to the driver. Ruth slumped in the other corner of the cab, not looking at him, her arms folded tightly against her chest to conceal the trembling of her body. The man was inclined to silence, too, eyes fixed thoughtfully out of the side window. But when the cab pulled up to the undistinguished entrance to the hotel, his face brightened.

At the door of Room 408, the man said, "You just relax, Mrs. Moody. You'll like my friend. He's a gentleman."

The gentleman was wearing a brocaded houserobe, and smoking a Turkish cigarette. He had made himself at home in Room 408, but the room had an air of sudden arrivals and quick exits. He was seated on the lumpy sofa, using an oblong coffee table as an impromptu desk. There were papers scattered in front of him and he was scrawling something on the top sheet, his tongue poking out of his mouth exploring his upper lip.

He looked up when Ruth and the sunburned man entered, his pale, youngish face suddenly cordial. He finished what he was writing, put down the pen, and invited them inside.

"You must be Ruth Moody," he said pleasantly. "Come sit on the sofa. It's the only comfortable thing in the place." He looked at the other man. "Why don't you fix Mrs. Moody a drink?"

"Sure. What would you like, Mrs. Moody?"

"Could I have some coffee?"

"Certainly," the gentleman said; he nodded to the sunburned man to get it. The man went to a table still cluttered with the remains of a hotel breakfast.

"Now, then, Mrs. Moody." The gentleman leaned back, and folded his hands over one knee. "Did my friend tell you very much about our plan?"

"No."

"That's just as well. Let me outline it for you."

He put out his cigarette.

"It's very simple," he continued airily, watching the other man place the coffee before her. "We happen to know that you're a kleptomaniac, Mrs. Moody. Now, now. Don't get upset over it. Both my friend and I are aware that doesn't mean you're a criminal. We respect your illness. Don't we?"

The sunburned man nodded.

"So," the gentleman said, "we'd like to make you a little offer. We hope you won't refuse, because if you do—"

"I told her, Harry."

"Good. Then I needn't go into that part. But the important thing I want you to remember, Mrs. Moody, is that no matter what happens, you're safe. Do you understand that? You can't be arrested for what we want you to do."

She gasped. "Arrested?"

"Yes. You see, legally, you're not liable for your little thefts. Surely, you've found that out already. You steal because you *have* to; no other reason. If you're caught—well, you merely return what's been stolen, and that's that."

"I don't understand this." Her voice was going shrill, and she fought to control it.

"Please. Let me explain. We know that you've been picked up three times."

She sipped the lukewarm coffee, her arm trembling as she raised the cup.

"This means that you're already a recognized klepto, Mrs. Moody. The stores and the police know all about you. If you were caught stealing something else—something, shall I say, a little more valuable than spools of thread . . ."

Her eyes widened, and the other man chuckled.

"I think you see our point now, Mrs. Moody. Now let me explain our plan in detail."

He picked up a sheet of paper from the coffee table.

"Here is exactly what you have to do. At twelve-fifteen tomorrow afternoon, you're to enter a shop called Travell's, on Forty-seventh Street. You may not know the place; it's a rather *soignée* jewelers, not exactly Tiffany's perhaps but well-recognized in its own right. You are to approach a certain counter, which I will diagram for you, and engage the attention of the salesman. You will ask to see a certain tray—I'll designate that, too—and then, a moment or so after you are examining that tray, there will be a disturbance in the store."

The short man laughed, with much enjoyment.

The gentleman went on: "It's ten to one the salesman will leave you alone with the tray since the disturbance will occur nearby. In any event, his attention will be drawn away from the business in hand long enough for you to take the pin without his noticing. In either case, you'll merely pick up the diamond sparkler on the upper right-hand corner and walk out the door. Simple as that."

Ruth Moody's skin went damp and cold.

"You needn't run, you understand. Merely walk out the door. As you come outside, you will see a man with a yellow cannister, collecting funds for Children's Welfare. You just drop the diamond pin in the opening on the top of the cannister, and walk to the corner. There will be a taxi waiting there; it's a hack stand. You will get in, and give him your home address." He leaned back and smiled. "And that's all there is to it."

She couldn't say anything. She looked towards the door, and then the window, aimlessly. She picked up the coffee cup but the liquid was cold and tasteless.

"I can't do it," she whispered. "I can't do such a thing."

"As I said before," the gentleman said smoothly, "you're safe—you have absolutely nothing to lose, Mrs. Moody. If you're stopped before you reach the exit, simply give yourself up. When Travell's learns of your—idiosyncracy, no harm will come to you. You know that. It'll be just another —medical incident. And that's all."

"I couldn't! I wouldn't have the nerve!"

The gentleman smiled again. "Nerve, Mrs. Moody? Now, really!"

He looked at the short man.

"Where did you say Mr. Moody worked?"

Grinning, the sunburned man reached into his coat.

Ruth said, "All right. Tell me exactly what I have to do."

The facade of Travell's was fastidiously designed, but unpretentious. One gem per window seemed to be the limit, but each needed no expert's eye or jeweler's loupe to proclaim its value. Ruth Moody, wearing her best dress, her good coat, and her newest hat, walked through the front entrance and felt like the thief she was going to be.

She recognized the store layout quickly from the comprehensive sketch the gentleman had shown her the day before. Some fifteen to twenty counters, each under the stewardship of a genteel salesman in a dark suit and silvery gray tie; a ceiling that rivaled a cathedral's, with a reverent hush to match. About a dozen people were paying their respects to the gems in the various showcases.

Ruth went to the counter that had been described to her. The salesman bowed slightly as he asked if he might be of service.

God help me, Ruth whispered to herself. "This tray," she said softly, supporting her nervous body with both hands against the counter. "The one on the second shelf. May I see it, please?"

"Certainly, Madam!" He reacted as if her taste were remarkable. He unlocked the rear of the case, and produced a velvety tray that flashed brilliant, blinding stars in her eyes.

"Some of the loveliest stones in our collection," the man said enthusiastically. "Did you have anything particular in mind?"

"I'm not sure." Her eyes went to the spectacular sparkler on the top row. *What's going to happen now?* she asked herself.

The answer came almost immediately. Not ten feet from where she stood, a gentleman in a topcoat with a velvet collar, and a homburg with a pearl-gray band, suddenly cried out some word that might have been "Heavens!" But his cry was lost in the unnerving sound—terrifying, in this place—of smashing glass. She saw the salesman's face whiten by shades when the noise came.

The gentleman in the homburg had been carrying an umbrella, with a heavy metal handle. He had swung it about, far too carelessly, and the motion had smashed the glass.

"Excuse me—!"

The salesman paused a split instant as if to take up the tray, then he rushed to the scene. Ruth heard the commotion and it was five precious seconds after he had gone that she recalled what she had to do. Her hand darted out and closed around the huge diamond pin in the upper right-hand corner of the tray. She slipped the gem into her coat pocket and began the long walk to the exit.

It was only some fifteen yards, but she was exhausted by the time the door swung behind her. The street was bright with sunshine, and the people were walking briskly by. There was laughter, and the click of heels, and many normal, everyday noises to give her renewed confidence. But she was frightened. When she saw the familiar sunburned face, and heard the jingle of coins in a cannister, she was actually grateful.

"Help the Children's Fund, lady?" He grinned at her.

"Yes," Ruth said dreamily. "Yes, of course." She deposited her contribution.

"There's a cab on the corner," the man said quietly, shaking the can. "Go home, Mrs. Moody."

"Yes," Ruth said.

As he turned to go, in the other direction, she saw an elderly lady drop a quarter in the cannister, and the sunburned face beamed with gratitude.

She got into the taxi but couldn't remember her own address until they were halfway up the street.

When Ralph Moody returned home that night, he found his wife in tears.

"Honey! What is it? What's wrong?"

"Oh, Ralph—"

His face darkened. "It happened again? Is that it?"

She moved her head, miserably.

"What was it this time?" he said, trying to keep the anger out of his voice. "What did you take?"

"Travell's," she sobbed.

"What?"

"Travell's. The jeweler's—"

"No, Ruth! Not *jewelry*—"

"You don't understand. I didn't *take* it. I *stole* it, Ralph. Don't you see? I *stole* something—"

After a while, when his anger subsided, gentle persuasion drew the whole story from her.

"I was so frightened," she said. "I didn't know what to do." She clutched his sleeve. "Ralph, I'm going to do what you and mother suggest. I'm going to see a doctor."

"Maybe it's too late for a cure," he replied. "This isn't a spool of thread or a handbag you took, Ruth. This is something valuable—God only knows *how* valuable."

"But they forced me to do it! They blackmailed me into it!"

"Is that what we're going to tell the police?"

"Police?"

"Of course. We have to call them, Ruth. Don't you see that?"

"Why? Why must we?"

"Because it's dangerous not to. If you were recognized—if that salesmen can give your description—then things will look worse than they really are. Don't you see that? We must call them!"

As he dialed the operator Ruth said: "But, Ralph—what if they don't believe me?"

Captain Samuel Wright, a graying, intelligent policeman, wasn't that incredulous. But his words of advice weren't encouraging when Ruth Moody told her story.

"Listen, Mrs. Moody. If you're holding back anything, don't. I'm not saying your story is a phony. My own subtle viewpoint is it's too cockeyed to be phony. But I could be wrong, dead wrong. Now, if you could *identify* these men—"

Ruth's husband said hotly, "Why should she lie about this? What does she have to gain?"

The Captain shook his head. "Uh-uh. That's no argument. She *could* stand to gain a diamond, a diamond worth maybe eight to ten grand. She could be double-crossing her accomplices. She could have figured that she had been spotted in Travells, so she's playing it safe with this screwy story." He held up a hand. "I don't say that's what happened. But I don't sit on the judge's bench, Mr. Moody. I'm a policeman."

"But it's true," Ruth said plaintively. "So help me, it's the truth."

"It's a heck of a way to pull a robbery, though. You'll have to admit that. How many people are going to believe it your way?" He lifted his wide shoulders in a gesture of doubt.

He paced the floor a moment.

"If you could only give me a better description. Except for one being sunburned, we got nothing to work with, really. You say they looked 'ordinary.' "

"But you checked that hotel, you know they were in that room."

"We only know *somebody* took the room, Mrs. Moody. Somebody who signed the register as a Mr. Fred Johnson, from Cleveland. We have no way of knowing whether it's an alias or not, now that the guy's checked out."

"But doesn't that prove—"

"It doesn't prove a thing. They might have colored their hair, changed their appearance. The sunburn, for instance —that's not going to last too long." He chewed his lip.

Ralph snapped his fingers. "The thousand dollars! They promised to mail Ruth a thousand dollars if she played along. Wouldn't that prove at least that my wife's innocent?"

"Don't count on that thousand, Mr. Moody. If your wife's telling the truth, you'll never hear a peep out of those guys again."

The Captain sat down, his face strained. "Okay! So maybe you're right. So maybe it's a new dodge. Maybe these guys can pull these 'safe' robberies of theirs all over the place. Maybe one of them works in a department store, and has access to the names of recognized kleptos—"

"Couldn't we check the stores? Identify the employees?"

"You know how many people work in those places? You're asking for an awful lot, Mr. Moody."

The tears were coming again and Ruth reached for her purse and a tissue. She applied the corner of it to her damp eyes.

Something inside her purse caught her attention as she was about to shut it.

She took the object out and stared at it. Then she turned it on its side and studied it again.

When she looked up once more her eyes were bright and miraculously dry.

"Captain!—"

"Yes, Mrs. Moody?"

"You need better identification. Would the name of the man in the hotel room help?"

"His *name?*" The Captain put his hands on his hips. "Are you kidding? You can really tell me his *name?*"

"I can. I can!" Ruth said. Then she started to laugh. The sound of it frightened her husband until he realized that it was genuine, honest mirth.

"Here," she said, handing him the object from her purse. "I don't know why I did—but I did. I took it from that hotel room yesterday."

The Captain turned the object over in his hand. It was a fairly high-priced fountain pen, gold, with a black cap. He peered closely at the gold letters engraved on the side: *Harrison V. Moyer.*

He grinned at Ruth, and went to the telephone. He used the end of the pen to dial headquarters.

MAKE YOUR PITCH

by Borden Deal

I WAS DOING REAL GOOD, working phones for Morgen & David Circus. Working phones, you're out ahead of the circus, selling tickets with a cold turkey telephone pitch under the auspices of the local organization. If you're a good pitchman, you can make lots of money with a setup like that. And believe me, I was making money. I had a powder-blue convertible, plenty of fancy threads, and all the circus tickets I needed to interest those small-town girls with stars in their eyes.

It was our last day for this town and I had just finished my shift on the phones. I decided to get a bite to eat before I loaded the convertible and took off. While I was collecting my day money, Jim Watson said, "Slim, you going to be with us on the next deal?"

"I've been on the phones so long they ring in my ears all night long," I said. "I may just do a quick walk-away and see you later on in the season."

"We're booked solid all the way to Florida," Jim said. "We need a good man like you."

"I'll let you know," I told him. "I feel like being fancy-free for a while."

He laughed. "There's nothing fancier and freer than a phone man," he said. "What are you looking for, Slim?"

"I'm just looking," I said. "Just looking."

There was a pretty good restaurant just a block away from the hotel. I walked down the small-town street, not paying much attention to anything except the girls. All the small towns are alike, north and south, east and west, and I think I've been in all of them, looking for the buck. But the women . . . they always know when you're a stranger in town. I don't know how they know it. But there is a speculation in the way they look at you that's always exciting, north or south, east or west. If you've got free circus tickets in your pocket, that makes you not just a stranger, but a special kind of stranger. You're show business. And they love the idea of show business.

I found a booth in the restaurant and had just ordered my dinner when this woman sat down opposite me. You know the kind of woman that reaches her perfection at thirty-five? Most of them have had their best days by the time they're eighteen or twenty. But once in a while there'll be one who isn't very much at eighteen, who's only a little better at twenty-five, but by the time she's thirty-five she's all that a man could ever hope to behold. This was one of them.

She was not tall, about five-two, I guess, and she was better dressed than most small-town women. She had something of the flair that you don't usually see except in the big cities. Her hair was ash-blonde and there was a special something in her face that I've learned to look for and to appreciate when I find it. I couldn't say just what it is, but it tells you that here's a woman who's not owned by any man.

"I want to talk to you, if you don't mind," she said.

I looked at her left hand. She had a gorgeous diamond. "I'm available," I said, with a flick of excitement inside me.

"You're with the circus phone crew?" she said.

"Yes," I said. "At least up until five minutes ago. I don't know whether I'll be with them tomorrow or not." She didn't seem to be the kind of woman who'd be interested in the kind of man I am. But you never can tell. "What's on your mind?" I said boldly. "Want some circus tickets?"

"No," she said. She reached out one hand to the glass of ice water beside my plate. She did not drink from it but began turning the glass around and around.

I always look at a woman's hands. You can tell a lot about a woman from the quality of her hands. It's a lot better than looking at their faces, because any woman can work sheer magic with a face. But there's not much you can do with hands. She had a firm, muscular hand, not too large. You could tell that she took care of them. The fingers were shorter than usual for the length of her palm so that her hands were square-looking. All in all, the most interesting hand I had seen in a long time.

She looked up at me from the glass. It was the first time I'd had a direct view of her eyes. They were hazel, flecked with green. Interesting eyes. Interesting hands. Interesting woman.

"No," she said. She turned the glass another careful circle, not taking her eyes from mine. Her voice was lower now, huskier, as though she found the words rather difficult to say. "I want you to kill a man."

It jarred me. I'd expected anything in the world except that simple, blunt statement. For just a minute, then, looking at her, I wasn't seeing a woman any more. It was only a flick of a second and then she was back again and somehow she was more desirable than she had been before. But the shock was still cold in the pit of my stomach. To cover it up I leaned back in the booth and looked at her.

"That's not my pitch," I said. "You've got me wrong, lady."

Her eyes were cold on my face and I wondered where the warmth had gone. "Making money is your pitch, as you call it, isn't it?" she said.

"Well, yes," I said. "I do like to make money."

She was leaning over the table now, straining toward me, and her voice was tenser and huskier than it had been before.

"Then how would you like to make twenty-five thousand dollars?"

That was enough money for the sound of it to be as strong a shock to me as her first declaration. I looked down at my plate, then I pushed it away from me. Suddenly I didn't want to eat any more. Then I looked up at her again, feeling her watching me before I could see her eyes.

"Lady," I said. "I'm a talker. I've been talking all my life. I can sell you anything there is to be sold. I can do a carny pitch; or a phone pitch, or I can sell neckties on the street. If you want a man talked to death, I'm the man who can do the job for you. But I gather that's not what you had in mind."

"No," she said. "You can't talk this man to death."

"Who is he?" I said.

"My husband," she said.

"Is it necessary to kill him?" I said. "Couldn't you just leave him? That would be simpler all the way around. I've got a blue convertible out there in the street."

"No," she said. "He has money."

I shook my head. "You'll have to get you another boy," I said. "This just isn't my racket, baby."

Her eyes flinched at the sound of the word "baby." I'd called her "lady" before. But there is a certain intimacy which springs up between two people quietly discussing cold-blooded murder.

"Don't forget the twenty-five thousand dollars," she said.

"I'm not likely to forget anything," I said. "Why me? Surely there's some local talent."

"That's just what's wrong," she said. "Local talent won't do. I want a man who's here today and gone tomorrow. A man I'll never see again, this town will never see again. And you're leaving soon, aren't you?"

"In just about five minutes," I said.

She leaned forward again. "You could do it tonight," she said. "No one would ever suspect you. There would be nothing to tie us together. And you'd have twenty-five thousand dollars in your pocket."

"You've got it?" I said.

She looked around the restaurant, then she opened her bag, tilting it toward me. It was a big bag. I could see the tight green clutter of bills inside, bulging the bag. When I saw the money a cold excitement started deep down in that part of me I hadn't been able to fill with the food on my plate. For the first time I began to think that it might happen. I could see what she meant. A bold move by a stranger who had a reason to be in town and a reason to be leaving might very well baffle the local meatheads.

I looked around the restaurant. "Suppose someone has seen us here?" I said.

"That's a chance I had to take," she said steadily. "But it's the only risk." She cased the restaurant carefully. "I don't see anyone I know," she said. "This is not a place where I come usually."

"It would be smart to get out of here, though," I said.

"Yes," she said. "Then we can go into greater detail. I'll walk down the block. You can follow me and pick me up in your car. I know a place where I'm sure we can be alone."

Her eyes flickered when she said the word "alone" and I thought, *There may be more in this than the twenty-five thousand.* I liked the thought and, at the same time, I didn't.

"All right then," I said. "I'll pick you up. I'm not promising anything. But we can talk about it."

I still didn't know how it happened. I felt like the woman who looks utterly unapproachable; but, if you handle it right, all of a sudden she finds she's not discussing the basic question at all, but only whether it's going to be your apartment or hers. Murder is like sex; once the question is admitted, you can't go back to trivialities.

She stood up. She went out very quickly and I watched her go, seeing the way she walked, proud and high, like a lovely woman of thirty-five should walk. After she was gone I looked down at my plate again. But the food didn't interest me. There was something much more powerful than the appetite for food working inside me and I thought, *Slim, is this the sort of thing you can do, after all?*

I picked her up on a quiet street three blocks from the restaurant. She got into the car when I slowed. She did not speak except to give me the directions. We went out of town and turned off onto a graveled country road that wound up into the hills. I kept my eyes straight ahead, not wanting to look at her. I was still wondering if I really intended to kill a man for twenty-five thousand dollars.

At last she motioned toward a turn-out beside the road. We were on a high hill overlooking the town. We sat for a moment staring down into the sparse sparkle of lights. Small towns always look so lonely when you can see the space around them.

She turned her shadowy head and looked at me. "Well," she demanded. "Have you decided yet?"

"Just what did you have in mind?" I said carefully.

She shrugged her shoulders. "It's very simple, really," she said. "He won't be home until eleven tonight. You can be waiting in the living room for him. When he walks in you shoot him. After you're sure he's dead, you can break a window and leave. I will be in the bedroom. I'll give you ten minutes head start and then I'll call the police and report that a prowler has just shot my husband."

"Will ten minutes be enough?" I said.

"It will be if you start out of town immediately," she said. "After all, there'll be no visible reason for you to be the murderer. And you were leaving anyway."

"What about the money?" I said. "When do I get that?"

She opened her bag and took out the money. "Here's five thousand now," she said. "You get the other twenty thousand after he's dead."

She handed me the five thousand dollars' worth of the green stuff. My hand reached out almost of itself to take the bills. I held them crushed hard, feeling their smoothness and their power. I'd never had a chance at twenty-five thousand dollars in my life. I'd made money, sure, but it was always in little chunks here and there. Like any talker, I'd always been looking for the big one, feeling that sooner or later it would come along. Now it had, and I wondered whether I had guts enough to take it. Because it hadn't come the way I'd expected it. I'd expected to have a chance with a shill or a confidence game or a come-on, the kind of deal that fitted with my talents. But this was strictly action.

"Why do you want to kill him?" I said.

She did not turn her head to look at me. "See that ridge of hills on the other side of town?" she said.

"Yes," I said.

"I was born there," she said. "I'm a country girl. When I

was fourteen, I knew there was only one thing I wanted to do . . . live in a town with sidewalks and street lights and movie theaters. I wanted to live in a house with running water and electricity and a television set." She moved her shoulders in an indefinable way. "There were eight kids in our family," she said. "We lived in a house that had four rooms. So I came to town. I met Carl, and I married him."

"So you got what you wanted," I said. I eyed her quizzically.

"Yes," she said. "Now I intend to go on."

"How did you happen to marry your husband?" I said.

"I came to town when I was sixteen," she said. "On the first day I was here, I saw him drive by in a car. I could tell by the car and by the way he looked and the way he drove that this was the kind of man that I needed to marry." She dug into the bag for a pack of cigarettes. She took out a cigarette and lit it. She threw the match out of the window, a brief flame arcing through the darkness. "I found out where he ate supper every night," she said. "I got a job in that restaurant." She shrugged her shoulders.

I had watched her face across the darkness while she was talking and I knew that she was telling the truth. We sat still for a moment, then I leaned over and kissed her. She did not flinch, she did not push me away. She merely sat cold and still under the kiss until I stopped. I drew away from her.

"You're not the man I'm looking for now," she said.

So it was going to be strictly a cash proposition. I leaned away from her and stared out over the wheel. "I don't know whether cash is enough or not," I said.

"What else do you want?" she said. She knew what I wanted.

"You don't go with the deal?" I said.

"No," she said. "I told you. You're not the man."

"What are you going to do after it's over?" I said.

"I'll wait a while," she said. "It'll take time to get the money that will be in his estate. Then I will go to the city."

She took her eyes away from the distant sparkle of lights and looked at me. "Will you do it?" she said.

I took a deep breath. "Yes," I said.

It surprised me, too. There was a change in her face, as though she had not expected me to agree. But far back in my mind had been the thought that you only get one chance at the big one and, if I passed this time, it would never come my way again. There's a lot that a talking man can do with twenty-five thousand dollars. You can spend your life talking, but if you don't have the capital to back up your spiel and your ideas, you're nowhere. That's the way I'd always been. All I needed was some money to begin with. I would have it now, and I knew I could parlay it into a big bank roll. So it wasn't my kind of action. So I would fit myself to the deal, instead of making the deal fit itself to me.

"What about the gun?" I said.

She delved into that bottomless bag of hers and came up with a .32 revolver. She handed it to me, after wiping it carefully with a scarf from the bag.

"Take it with you when you leave," she said. "Ditch it somewhere a thousand miles away."

"You've got it all figured, haven't you?"

"Yes," she said. "Are you ready to go as soon as it's over?"

"I'll have to pick up my luggage at the hotel," I said. "My walk-away money is in my kick and, believe me, I won't need a road map."

"Take me back to town," she said. "Then you can follow me home so you can find the house again later on."

I started the engine, backed the car, and drove toward town. We were silent again, though we were the closest kind of partners two people can ever be. I felt closer to her than to any woman I'd ever known, even though our single kiss had been a nothing. We stopped on a dark street and she got out of the car.

"At ten-thirty, just come in the front door and wait in the living room," she said. "The house will be dark. He'll come in around eleven and then you can do the job."

She walked away quickly and I watched her going down the street, thinking that this town didn't have the faintest idea of the kind of woman they had adopted from their countryside. I almost wished that she was going with me, or that somewhere, sometime, we would meet again. But I knew that was no good. I was her tool, just like the money and the gun, and for my own purposes I was content to be her tool.

She got into a big car down the street and I followed her as she drove through the streets of the town. She went out a tree-shaded avenue, turned right, and pulled into the driveway of a big house. It was brick, long and low, and the grounds around it must have been at least an acre in size. The husband had money, all right.

After she had gone into the house, I drove back to the hotel to collect my luggage. Going into the lobby, I met Jim Watson coming out.

"Jim," I said. "I've made up my mind. I'm cutting out for a while."

"Well, they come and they go," Jim said cheerfully. "See you around, Slim, boy." He went on.

That's the way it is. Nobody is surprised when a phone man comes or when a phone man goes. They pay every day, so you can be free to leave any time you want to. I was one of Jim's favorite workers but, the way he'd acted, you couldn't tell whether he cared ever to see me again. And, with luck, he never would.

I didn't get fidgety as the time moved on to the big moment. I seemed to get harder inside, colder, more sure of myself. I had expected to be nervous, if not frightened, but sitting in the car and casing the house from a distance for a few minutes while I smoked a cigarette, I found my hands as steady as a rock.

I got out of the car and sauntered up the walk to the house as though I were an honored guest. I did not ring the bell. I pushed the door and it was unlocked. I stepped inside a small foyer and looked into the dark living room. I would have a short wait, then I would kill a man. I would collect my money and I would go into my brand-new world.

Everything was set up just the way we had planned. I

touched the gun in my pocket, then I walked into the dark living room. I stopped in the middle of the floor space and looked around, planning the best place to wait for the man to come. As I turned, surveying the room, the lights suddenly blazed on. I ducked, my hand going swiftly toward my pocket. The man stood in the bedroom doorway, the gun in his hand pointed unwaveringly toward me.

He was a stocky, powerful man, considerably older than I was. There was gray in his hair, lines in his face. On his shirt was pinned the badge of a lawman.

I was utterly stunned. I stood still, my hand arrested in its motion toward the gun. He watched me for a moment, then he began walking toward me. I wanted to run, but I knew he would kill me if I moved. I didn't have time to wonder what had gone wrong for behind him, standing in the bedroom doorway, I saw the woman.

"You're right on time," he said. "Very commendable, young man."

"What do you mean?" I said. "I came to . . ."

"I know why you came," he said. "You came to kill me. You thought."

I looked from him to the woman. "Listen," I said. "What's the deal here?"

He laughed. He came closer to me, then motioned her to come around him. "Get the money," he said.

She did not avoid my eyes as she walked toward me, careful not to block the gun. She folded my lapel back so she could get my wallet out of the breast pocket. She opened the wallet deftly and extracted the money. Then she took the gun out of my pocket.

"Wait a minute," I said. "Some of that money is mine."

"Some of it was yours," the man said. "It's hers, now."

She counted the money swiftly. "It's all here," she said. "My five thousand, and almost three thousand more."

I was baffled and angry. "Listen," I said. "Just what the devil . . ."

He laughed again. I was beginning to get tired of the sound of his laugh. "Don't you know yet?" he said.

"I sure don't," I said.

"This is Clara's little game," he said. "She likes to work it once in a while. It gives her pin money, a feeling of independence. You know how a wife likes to have a little money of her own."

"You mean . . ." I said. "All that talk about . . ."

"Yes," he said. "Clara has used several stories. But that one is really the best, don't you think?"

I looked at her. There was a small smile on her face as she looked down at the money. She looked up at her husband.

"It's a good haul, Carl," she said. "Not many of them have that much money on them. We caught him just right."

"What's the tin badge for?" I said. "Do you think that gives you the authority to . . ."

"I'm the Sheriff of this county," he said mockingly. "Didn't she tell you?"

"No," I said. "It seems there's a lot she didn't tell me. But if you're the Sheriff . . ."

He sat down in a chair, holding the gun carelessly pointed toward me. "I love my wife," he said. "When she married me, I knew it was because of my money. I told her then I'd do anything in the world for her. And I meant it."

Her eyes were on him as he talked. "I love you, Carl," she said. "You know that, don't you?"

He chuckled. "Sure," he said. "You love me. Because I let you play your little games."

"I'm going to Florida next week," she said. "I'll bet it all on the horses and the dogs." Her voice was very happy.

I stood stiff and straight in the living room. "So what happens now?" I said.

He looked at me idly. "If you're smart, you'll blow this town," he said. "And fast. You really have no other recourse."

"Yes," I said bitterly. It was beginning to sink in. I'd been suckered by a weird kind of badger game. "Yes, I guess you're right."

But I didn't move. I kept looking from one to the other of them. Her eyes were gleaming as her hands shuffled the money. She began putting it into that big bag.

"Just a moment, darling," he said. "Five thousand of that is mine."

"Carl," she said in a wheedling voice.

"Give me the five," he said.

"So you stake her, too," I said with the bitterness still in my voice.

"Of course," he said.

She came to the side of his chair and tucked the five grand into his coat pocket. She gave him the .32, dropping it in on top of the money. She sat down on the arm of his chair, her arm across his shoulders. They both looked at me.

"You'd better get going," he said.

My mind was running frantically around the edges of the problem. I knew I was caught. There was no way out. He could shoot me and get away with it. He could put me in jail. I had broken into his house with a gun in my pocket, and she would back him up all the way. It was as pretty a trap as a stupid man could ever walk into.

"All right," I said. "I'm on my way."

I began walking toward the door. I knew this was a place where my gift of talking wouldn't do a bit of good. This was no place for a talker to be. Then I stopped. I turned and looked at them. They made a cozy domestic picture, except for the gun in his hand. Her arm was across his shoulders and her fingers were riffling his hair.

"Sheriff," I said. "I hope she never tells you how far she had to go to get me to do the job." I saw him stiffen.

I went on very quickly. "You know, some men will kill," I said. "But most men will not kill for money alone. It takes love, too."

I was gone, then, fast out the front door and down the walk. I began to run when I hit the sidewalk and I did not stop until I had reached the car.

As I started the motor, I heard the first shot.

THE LITTLE THINGS

by Ed Lacy

PUFFING CONTENTEDLY on his pipe, Chief Paul Polo waited for the 6:45 P.M. train and for Harry Morris. A large man, now running to middle-age lard, Polo barely knew Morris but he felt proud to be waiting for the man.

His interest had nothing to do with the news item; Polo had been a cop for too many years to bother about his name appearing in print. But this was a different crime story. Polo had single-handedly righted a miscarriage of justice, and he was pleased because it confirmed his concept of police work: keep digging and the solution to any crime *has* to appear, even after nearly ten years.

Opening the local paper (the editor was certain the wire services would pick it up, give Polo national fame) he re-read the piece:

> CARRINGTON COVE. Harry Morris is due home today from State Prison, where he was serving a life sentence for murder. His freedom is important, of course, but of far greater importance is the tremendous example of police work by our own Chief Paul Polo which this freedom represents.
>
> Due to the rapid growth of your community in the past ten years, few people remember Mr. Morris. When Carrington was merely an unknown fishing village, Harry Morris was the first artist to settle here. Chief Polo recalls him as a ". . . very quiet fellow, almost a hermit. He kept to his shack out in the Cove, working hard at his paintings. We later learned Mr. Morris had quit a good job with an ad agency in New York City to devote himself to his art."

A year after Morris had settled in Carrington, Mrs. Lucy Moore, a striking blonde summer tourist, was found shot to death in her cottage. Mr. Morris readily admitted he had not only struck up a friendship with the striking blonde, but that he had been Mrs. Moore's lover. He claimed he had visited her on the night of the murder, told her that their affair was over, and stated that the break had been peaceful and friendly. Morris then said he had returned to his shack, about a half mile from the Moore cottage, and gone to bed. He denied ever owning a gun. Due to his hermit-like existence, Harry Morris could not prove he had been in his shack at the time of the shooting. Mr. Moore, who was away on a selling trip, had an iron alibi. Chief Polo, then an ordinary officer, arrested Morris, and at his trial Harry Morris was convicted of murder in the first degree on circumstantial evidence, sentenced to life imprisonment. The murder gun was never found.

At the time, Carrington was far from the sophisticated art center it is today, and the fact that Morris had relations with the dead woman convicted him in the eyes of the village. To his credit, Police Officer Polo always felt there was more than a reasonable doubt about Morris' guilt. "Somehow, I couldn't see him as a man of violence. Nor could I believe the State's theory that Mrs. Moore had refused to end the affair, threatened to become a pest, hence Morris shot her."

Over the years, in his own time and with his own money, and unknown to Harry Morris, Chief Polo dug into the case. One year Chief Polo and Mrs. Polo spent their vacation in Los Angeles where the Chief discovered that Lucy Moore had not been married to Mr. Moore but was in fact a Mrs. Donald Jackson.

It took more years for Chief Polo to track down Donald Jackson, who moved about a good deal. Six months ago, Polo learned Jackson was in a Colorado T.B. hospital. At his own expense Chief Polo flew there and questioned Jackson as to his whereabouts on the night of the murder, nine long years ago. A very sick man, Jackson refused to talk. Chief Polo returned to Carrington, but every week or so he would phone Jackson, reminding him an innocent man was in the state pen. Finally, three weeks ago, shortly before he died, Donald Jackson signed a confession that he had been in a jealous rage at Lucy running off with Mr. Moore, had driven to Carrington on the night of the murder and killed her.

Today, Harry Morris returns to Carrington, thanks to Chief Polo's tireless efforts to see true justice done. In these days, with headlines of police corruption and brutality blaring across our country, Carrington proudly salutes our Police Chief, Paul Polo.

Polo shoved the paper back into his pocket. He'd always worked hard at his job, was proud of his shield, yet the article left him slightly embarrassed. He didn't know of any other way of working except to do his best.

The 6:45 came in, and it was easy to spot Harry Morris among all the sunburned tourists. Morris was thin and pale, white hair above a still sensitive face. He held himself lean and erect in the cheap suit, holding a small canvas bag in his left hand.

The two men stared at each other for a moment and grinned. Morris said, the deep voice in contrast to his sickly color, "Well, I don't have to ask who you are. I fully realize how inadequate the words 'Thank you' must sound, but truly I say thank you, Chief."

"Only doing my job," Polo mumbled, more embarrassed than ever. "Look, Morris—Harry, I don't know what your plans are. I guess you'll sue the State for false arrest, but that will take time and . . ."

"No sir, I shall not sue. While I can't honestly say I enjoyed my years of confinement, it did give me a chance to experiment, to evaluate my work. I'm not an oil painter, have no sense of color. But I am a good engraver, an etcher, and I can hardly wait to start work."

"As you'll see, Carrington is far from the little wide-spot-in-the-road you remember. Your house and land were sold long ago for taxes. What I am saying is, it will take time for you to find a job, and you're welcome to room with me and Maude. For free."

Morris flashed a big smile. "Thank you again, Chief, but that won't be necessary. I had $6,000 in the bank at the time of my arrest. By now, with interest, I have over $9,-000. I'll take a room at the hotel for a week, while I find a quiet place to live, then start my work."

"I have my car. Can I drive you any place?"

"Chief, I'd rather walk, see how the town looks. I've been looking forward to this walk for a long time." Morris shook Polo's meaty hand again and then started down the short and lonely stretch of road which met Carrington's main street, coming alive with lights in the twilight.

Harry Morris had almost reached the main street when a car drew alongside, a rifle bullet tore the side of his head open. A young man jumped out and took the cheap canvas bag, quickly ran his hands through the dead man's pockets, then leaped back into the car, and sped away.

Pointing to the supper table, Maude Polo said, "Really, Paul, this is the third night in a row you've only toyed with your supper. I'm too good a cook to be treated this way. You have to stop worrying over Harry Morris' killing."

"It isn't exactly worry," Paul said, poking at the meat before him with his fork. "You know me, I never bring my job home. The thing that bothers me is the unfairness. An innocent man does ten years on a bum rap and before he has a chance to enjoy his freedom, sort of taste it, he's shot down. It sort of makes a fool of justice."

"You are worried or you'd be eating. Paul, you'll find the killers. You'll dig and dig away at the facts until you come up with the guilty one."

"I have been digging, like a frightened mole, and haven't even hit a smell of paydirt. Harry Morris didn't have any relatives, so that rules out a family grudge. The killing was in the old gangland style but at State Prison they insist Harry was a loner, wasn't mixed up with any of the punks in there."

"I've been thinking about it myself," Maude said, starting to put the food away. "He told you he was interested in engraving. Could Harry have been mixed up with counterfeiters?"

Paul shook his rough, gray head. "I checked on that, too. The warden insists he didn't have any cons with a record for queer money in State, said they'd be in a Federal pen. Besides, they kept a special eye on Morris' etchings for that very reason. You mention engraving and everybody thinks of counterfeiting. No, Maude, I've been doing a lot of thinking and sifting of facts, and there are only two ways in which Harry Morris differed from the average man released from jail: he was an artist, which I don't think means anything, far as the killing goes, and he had $9,000 in the bank. Could be the money is the key. There are three banks in Carrington and tomorrow . . ."

"But ten years ago there was only the Carrington Savings Bank," Maude cut in.

"That's right. Well, tomorrow I'll go in and have a talk with Ed Johns. Of course, Harry could have had the money in a big city bank someplace, and there must be a thousand of them. But we'll see. Maybe Harry had a lot more than nine grand."

The next morning Chief Polo sat across the desk from Ed Johns, president of Carrington Savings. Johns was an imposing man, looking like the type who indeed had twice been mayor of Carrington. Polo explained why he was there, and Ed said, "I'll look in the files myself, Paul. I remember Morris. He used to pester me to cash checks for him, now and then. Personal checks on some city bank, maybe New York City. This was a dozen years ago, so I can't recall all the details. But I remember it because I kept after him, at the time, to open an account. We were a small bank then, needed all the new accounts we could get. Also, putting a check through for Morris meant the bookkeeping of waiting for it to clear. I can't recall if he ever did open an account. But I'll see."

Chief Polo sat back in the neat leather chair, admiring the swank office and how pretty Edith Bloom, Ed's secretary, had grown. Polo remembered her as a baby in her father's grocery store. He said, "You're sure a fine-looking gal, Edith. Guess you'll be getting married soon."

"Next June, soon as Mickey Gans graduates Syracuse. He has a job waiting for him out in California and I can hardly wait to move."

"Our Chamber of Commerce would take a dim view of such talk. What's wrong with Carrington?"

Edith grinned. "I love Carrington. It's this job." She lowered her voice. "Of course, I expect to work for awhile after I marry Mickey, but I don't want to work here. Old grumpy is a slave driver. Never gives me a second off. Do this, do that, get me this or . . ."

Ed Johns returned, shaking his balding head. "Nothing, Paul. Our records go back eleven years and Harry Morris never had an account. Sorry I can't be of much help. Say, Paul, you haven't been out on my new 45-foot cruiser yet, have you? Great for weekend fun."

"Nope. She's a pretty boat."

"Any weekend you want, we'll go fishing. For the big babies, thirty or forty miles offshore."

"Thanks, Ed. I'm kind of busy now but when I get some free time, I'll take you up on that."

Leaving the office Chief Polo waved at Jed Wert, the guard, nodded to the various tellers as he made for the door. He asked Joe Rogers how the new baby was, winked at Lawrence Henry, who once had been Carrington's sole juvenile delinquent with his habit of "borrowing" rowboats. He stopped to ask Fred Scales, "Think you have a chance in the state drag races?"

"I hope so, Mr. Polo. I just put a Ferrari souped-up engine in my buggy; she can make one hundred miles per hour before I turn on the ignition!"

"Well, be careful," Polo said, going on to the last window to ask Mark Gilutin, "How's your wife doing?"

"She's coming along real fine, Chief, but the docs say it will take another few months in the rest home."

"You've had more than your share of tough luck, Mark.

First your poor mama and now your wife. Tell Mary I asked for her."

Back in his own small office Polo put through a call to the state banking department. When he explained what he wanted, he was told, "Legally we can ask for the records of every bank in the state, but have you any idea of what a job that would be? It would keep our entire staff going full time for months. Chief, you'd have to secure a court order to make us do it, and quite frankly we'd fight it. Too expensive."

Picking away at the veal chops that evening, he told Maude, "Nobody's interested in *one* man, that's what's wrong with the world today. I even went over to see Judge Haff and he kept saying it would cost the state about $100,000 to go over the records of all the banks for the last ten years. I told him you can't equate justice in terms of money."

"Don't tell me Larry Haff refused to give you the court order?" Maude asked, voice rising.

"Well, not point-blank. He merely tried to talk me out of it. Anyway, I'd have to go to a higher court than his."

Maude said, "Now eat your meat, Paul, I won't heat it up again. It does seem odd Harry Morris wouldn't have kept an account in our bank. I mean, go through all the fuss of having them cash a check on another bank whenever he needed eating money."

"I was thinking the same thing. Larry Haff told me some interesting things about bank accounts. Did you know that if a savings account lies dormant for ten years, no money is ever put into it or withdrawn, it reverts to the State? Of course the owner can always collect his money from the State, if he shows up. Also . . ."

"And Harry Morris spent almost ten years in jail!" Maude put in. "You don't think Ed Johns would have forged Harry's name, withdrawn the money, thinking Morris would be in jail until he died?"

Chief Polo chewed on a mouthful of meat for a few seconds. Then he said, "I don't know. I can't see Ed, with his cars, his boat, his fine house, his standing in the community, I can't see him stealing $9,000. Why he must be worth a hundred thousand, at least. But it could have been one of the tellers; Joe Rogers has four kids now; Lawrence Henry—well, you know his record, maybe he hasn't outgrown his taking ways; Fred Scales said he put an expensive new motor in his hot rod; and Mark Gilutin, saddled with all those hospital bills. Any one of them might have withdrawn the money, removed all records of the account. That's why an investigation is so costly. They'd have to audit and balance the books for the last ten years."

"Paul, what are you going to do?"

"Try a bluff. I'm going to let it be known I have the court order for the records of every bank in the state to be examined, see if that flushes anybody out of our Carrington Savings."

The following day Chief Polo was in the bank to cash a small check, casually told the tellers about the time he had securing a court okay to examine the records of every bank in the state, added with a corny wink, "Watch your fingers, fellows, they'll probably start with this one."

Polo also quietly put a roadblock on the one highway leading out of Carrington. He himself kept an eye on the harbor. At 2 A.M. Ed Johns' big sedan, with Fred Scales driving, stopped at the dock. As Fred began unloading suitcases to take on board, Chief Polo stepped out of the shadows. Fred and Ed Johns tried to make a run for the boat, and Polo had to put a shot through the flying bridge windshield before they stopped.

As Polo told the reporters in the morning, "It wasn't only poor Harry Morris' money. They had been looting these dormant accounts for the last five years, confessed to having taken over $80,000. If nobody bothers with an account for ten years, it's a safe guess the party has died and the account is unknown to any possible heirs. So they were doing okay until they took Harry's account, because they never expected him to be released. But once he presented his bank book, the rest of their stealing would have come to light, so they murdered him, took the one link to them —his bankbook."

But that night as he sat back in his old chair, comfortably stuffed with a big supper, Maude asked, "Paul, how in the world did you suspect Ed Johns? Since you were watching his boat, you must have been pretty certain he was the one. Ed is a stuffed shirt, but I'd never take him for a crook."

Belching happily, Paul said, "It was being such a stuffed shirt that caused a little thing he did to make me suspicious of him. Ed always said an executive shouldn't move from behind his big desk. Yet when I asked if Morris had an account, Ed went to look up the records himself. That struck me as phony. He probably wanted to make certain no evidence of the account remained." Paul sighed. "You shouldn't have made stew, Maude, you know I can't resist it. And I shouldn't have tackled that last little hunk of pie. Like with Ed Johns, it's always the little things which trip the biggest crooks and gluttons."

HOLDOUT

by Jack Ritchie

NOT GUILTY," Henry Watson said stubbornly.

Stanley Vetter continued polling the jury. "Rothwell?"

"Guilty."

"Jenkins?"

"Guilty."

"Coleman?"

"Guilty," I said.

And then the eleven of us glared at Watson.

"Once again," Vetter said. "And on the twenty-sixth ballot, I might add, we stand eleven for conviction, one for acquittal."

I took a strained breath. "I think we are dealing with an idiot."

Watson got to his feet. "Now see here . . ."

Vetter quickly raised a hand. "Now, now, Watson, I'm sure Coleman didn't mean that."

"Of course, I meant it," I said stiffly. "Never in my experience have I encountered such an obstinate, stupidly . . . stubborn man."

Vetter lowered his voice and spoke in my ear. "We won't get anywhere by antagonizing him."

"We've tried being sweetly reasonable," I muttered. "And that hasn't done any good. We have attempted to appeal to his intelligence, but obviously that was futile from the start."

Vetter was a large man moulded for an easy chair. "Let's take this easy and not lose our tempers."

I glowered at Watson. "Do you *actually* believe that Duke O'Brien is innocent?"

He shifted uncomfortably. "Oh, I *think* he's guilty, all right. But you don't seem to understand my viewpoint. In my opinion, the state just hasn't *proved* that he murdered Matt Tyson."

"Maybe so, son," Vetter said. "But if that's your opinion, you're lonelier than a chaplain in the Russian army."

I spoke with acid patience. "Duke O'Brien and Tyson were the only ones in the room. It was the rear room of a tobacco store. An off-duty policeman happened to be in the shop purchasing a pipe when he heard the shot. He rushed to the back of the store and when he opened the door, he noted the following: Matt Tyson thoroughly dead on the floor, the smell of gunsmoke in the air, and Duke O'Brien in the process of exiting via the window. He pursued O'Brien through several alleys and fired a number of warning shots. It was either because of that . . . or because O'Brien ran out of wind . . . that the chase finally ended with O'Brien's surrender to the officer."

"But the police never found the murder weapon," Watson said obstinately.

Rothwell, a thin druggist who looked as though he had been born with a headache, took over the attack. "O'Brien was chased for blocks—through backyards and over fences. It was night, and during the chase he tossed the gun away. The police didn't search the area until morning." Rothwell appeared disgusted by that negligence. "What was the first thing O'Brien did when he was taken to the police station? He demanded to see his lawyer and the police allowed him to. And I'll tell you what O'Brien told his lawyer. He told him where he'd tossed the gun and the lawyer got one of Duke's boys to pick it up that night."

"But Duke claimed that he didn't have a gun."

"He was wearing a shoulder holster. An empty shoulder holster. Would he be wearing that if he hadn't been carrying a gun?"

"But Duke said that he *usually* carried a gun—he just forgot to take it along that night."

Rothwell closed his eyes for a moment. "The police found traces of gunpowder on O'Brien's right hand."

"I know," Watson admitted. "But O'Brien said that he'd been target shooting a couple of hours earlier. That's how it got on his hand."

Rothwell looked as though he wanted to cry; and he bit his lips.

There was a knock at the door and the court attendant's head and shoulders appeared. "The judge wants to know if you've reached a verdict yet."

I scowled. "Would we still be here if we had?"

He backed out. "You don't have to bite my head off. The judge just told me to ask."

Miss Jenkins, a determined school teacher, spoke to Watson as though he were in her third grade. "You do know that Duke O'Brien is a bad man, don't you?"

"Well . . . yes."

"He is a racketeer, isn't he?"

"I suppose so, but . . ."

"He controls the underworld of this city, doesn't he? Whether it's narcotics, or gambling, or . . ." She blushed slightly. "Or other things. He has control of them all?"

"Yes," Watson said desperately. "But he isn't being tried for *those* things. He's being tried for murder."

"Mr. Watson," Miss Jenkins said sternly. "You are a stubborn, stubborn man."

Watson appealed to us. "If Duke O'Brien is such a big operator . . . if he's got an *organization* . . . with killers and all that . . . why should he shoot Tyson himself? He could have had somebody else do the job for him and he could have been miles away with an alibi."

"It was a spur-of-the-moment thing," Rothwell said. "That tobacco store is just a coverup for a bookie joint or something like that, and he and Tyson got into some kind of an argument. O'Brien lost his head and shot Tyson. Did you expect witnesses?"

"No, but . . ."

"Mr. Watson, do you know what *circumstantial* evidence is?"

"Yes, but I still think that the state hasn't . . ."

I took over. "Let us for the moment assume that you are

a man of intelligence. Why did O'Brien run, if he was innocent?"

"He got panicky."

"What was his feeble story of what he claims happened?"

Watson rubbed his neck. "O'Brien said he and Tyson were just talking when a shot came through the open window."

I smiled tightly. "An open window? It was 38 degrees outside. Why would anybody want to keep a window open in that kind of weather?"

"O'Brien said the room was smoky."

"The prosecution established the fact that neither O'-Brien nor Tyson smoke."

"O'Brien said the room was smoky when he and Tyson went in."

"O'Brien said, O'Brien said," Rothwell snapped bitterly. "You believe everything O'Brien says. Why?" He leaned forward. "Do *you* intend to buy a *new* automobile if this is a hung jury, too?"

Watson's face went white. "See here, I won't be talked to that way. I demand an apology."

Vetter the peacemaker, held up a hand. "I think we're all pretty tired and we're all hungry. What do you say we take a break?"

We sent out for sandwiches and coffee.

Vetter, Rothwell, and I grouped around our coffee cups at one end of the long table.

Rothwell ate without enthusiasm. "Suppose this ends like the first trial?"

Vetter sighed. "Let's hope not."

Rothwell glowered at Watson eating alone. "*He* won't be stupid enough to buy a car. He'll keep the money hidden away until it's safe to spend it."

"Let's not jump to conclusions," Vetter said. "He might honestly believe that O'Brien hasn't been proved guilty."

This was the second time Duke O'Brien had been tried for the murder of Matt Tyson. The first trial had ended with a hung jury. Eleven for conviction, one for acquittal.

Three days after the jury had been dismissed, the juror holding out for acquittal had purchased a new automobile. It was something his neighbors noticed and it was something that did not escape the attention of the authorities either. It was also discovered that he had deposited five thousand dollars to his bank account a day previously.

The juror was under indictment now, and though he would admit to nothing, it was obvious that Duke O'Brien had managed to reach him with a bribe.

We waited until the courtroom attendant cleared the cups and saucers and then resumed our seats around the table.

Vetter spoke. "Mr. Watson, justice works in peculiar ways."

"It does?"

Vetter nodded. "You've read about racketeers going to prison, haven't you?"

"Of course."

"And you have noticed that it is very seldom that they are sent to prison because they have been tried for *racketeering*. They are usually put away because of something else—evasion of income taxes is common."

"Yes."

"And they are given unusually stiff sentences, aren't they? Ten years? Fifteen?"

Watson waited for the point.

Vetter smiled. "In the case of ordinary tax evaders, there is usually considerable leniency. A fine, perhaps, a suspended sentence, or occasionally a very short term in prison. But in the case of a racketeer, he is given the *maximum* sentence, the *maximum* fine."

Watson nodded.

"Then don't you see? The judge is not actually sentencing him for the evasion of income taxes, he is in effect sentencing him for *all* the crimes he knows he has committed —but which the authorities have been unable to prove he committed."

Watson sighed. "I know what you mean, however . . ."

"Even if you don't think that O'Brien has been proved

guilty of this particular crime, you certainly must know that he *is* guilty of many others. You would be finding him guilty of the *entire* life of crime he has lived."

"Yes," Watson agreed reluctantly. "But a prison sentence is one thing, and a . . . I mean that if we find him guilty, a death sentence is *mandatory* in this state."

Rothwell half-rose. "Is *that* why you won't find O'Brien guilty? Because he'll go to the chair?"

Watson avoided his eyes.

Rothwell's voice rose. "*Before* you were selected for this jury, you were *asked* if you had any objections to capital punishment. And evidently you didn't, or you wouldn't be in this room."

Watson colored. "Well, I didn't . . . don't. But . . . this Tyson wasn't exactly one of our better citizens . . . and O'-Brien was almost doing the world a favor . . ." He swallowed. "Don't you think that the death penalty is a little severe in this case?"

There was silence and then Vetter said, "Son, do you want a murderer walking around free in this world?"

"No. Of course not." He took a deep breath. "But suppose that we have a hung jury now. That doesn't mean that O'Brien will go free. The state will just try him again and he'll be found guilty the next time."

Miss Jenkins was shocked. "Mr. Watson, do you *realize* what you're saying? You actually think that O'Brien is guilty, but you want somebody *else* to do the . . . dirty work."

Vetter shook his head sadly. "So you think the state will try O'Brien again?"

Watson put a finger in his collar. "Why, of course."

Vetter smiled sadly. "It's possible, but I wouldn't bet on it. In theory the state can keep trying O'Brien indefinitely, until there's a verdict, one way or the other. But when there are *two* hung juries, the prosecutor's office begins to wonder. Does it really have enough of a case to convince a jury? Is it worth while going through all the trouble, the time, the expense just to try O'Brien again and maybe get *another* hung jury? Or even an acquittal? Or maybe the prosecutor just gets disgusted and says, 'If I can't find twelve jurors with the honesty and the *guts* to put O'Brien where he belongs, then the hell with it. We'll turn him loose. He's exactly what the citizens deserve. They've brought this on themselves.' "

Watson looked uncomfortable.

"There are other things that could happen," Vetter said. "Maybe the policeman who caught O'Brien will suddenly 'forget' what he saw. He's probably got mortgage payments like everybody else and if he thinks that O'Brien can keep buying his way out of the electric chair, he might decide that it's smart to get in on some of the money."

"Look, Watson," Rothwell said. "You wouldn't be sending O'Brien to the chair for just this one killing. Maybe he doesn't deserve the chair for getting rid of Tyson, but does he deserve to go *free?*"

"Son," Vetter said. "Do you think that this is the only time O'Brien's been responsible for somebody dying? Every time you read about somebody being found dead in the trunk of his own car, you know doggone well who was behind it."

"Anyway you look at it," I said vehemently, "O'Brien deserves to sizzle in the chair."

Watson winced.

"Mr. Watson," Miss Jenkins said quietly. "Do you have children?"

Watson nodded. "Two. The boy is fourteen. The girl seventeen."

"Do you think they'd be proud of you if you let O'Brien go free? If you shirked your duty?"

Watson said nothing.

Miss Jenkins went on. "You are aware of the narcotics traffic in this city, are you not? And how many *high-school* students have been lured into addiction by O'Brien and his kind?"

There was a long silence and then Watson looked up. He sighed. "You're right. All of you. I was being a . . . a coward."

Vetter beamed. "Let's make it formal. I'll call the roll."

When his turn came, Watson stood up. "Guilty," he said firmly.

Vetter nodded approvingly and continued. "Rothwell?"

Guilty."

"Jenkins?"

"Guilty."

"Coleman?"

"Not guilty," I said.

They stared at me.

I stood up. "It has suddenly struck me that we are violating one of the most elementary principles of justice. We are convicting O'Brien for what we *think* he is, rather than on the charge which brought him into court."

But that, of course, was not my actual reason for changing my vote.

As long as Watson had held out, everything would have been satisfactory. I would have preferred that *he* appeared responsible for the hung jury and I had continually antagonized and insulted him in the hope of bolstering his stubbornness.

But now Watson had changed his mind.

I regarded the eleven surprised jurors and realized that now I would have to begin working for my money.

I'd have to make it convincing.

After all, Duke O'Brien had given me ten thousand dollars to make sure there would be a hung jury.

THE LATE UNLAMENTED

by Jonathan Craig

THE CORPSE had come straight through the wall. Someone had opened the hatch on the coal chute out in the alley, shoved the man's body inside, and closed the hatch again. The body had slid down the chute, burst through the plywood cover at the other end, and fallen to the floor of what once had been an out-sized coal bin but which was now a bright, den-type room tricked out with what some Greenwich Villagers call "beginner's décor." There were splashy posters on the walls for bullfights in Spain and Mexico and slightly smaller posters for auto races at Le Mans and Nürburgring, a pink-dyed fishnet draped across one corner, a boatswain's chair suspended in another, and the usual scattering of unframed abstractions and ceramic wall-pieces. On the table there was even a straw-jacketed Chianti bottle with a stub of candle stuck in the neck and thick laps of tallow down the sides.

The DOA had been a tall, slope-shouldered young man with a thin, deeply tanned face a little too sharp-featured to be called handsome, and a small, crescent-shaped scar just above his right eyebrow.

"Any chance he could have got that head wound when he hit the floor in here?" I asked the assistant medical examiner who was kneeling beside the body for another look.

The M.E. shook his head. "He landed on his left shoulder and the left side of his head, Pete," he said. "That's obvious. But it was the clout in the *back* of his head that killed him—and that's something he had before he started down the chute."

"His neck broken?"

"No—and a broken neck he didn't need. I've rarely seen such a massive skull fracture, Pete. I can't imagine what could have inflicted it, but the bone is depressed in such a way that I'd say offhand it was something big and heavy and spherical. But I can tell you one thing for sure. He hasn't been dead more than two hours, if that." He snapped his bag shut and got to his feet. "You understand I'm saying all this strictly as doctor to cop, so you can get started on your investigation. *Officially,* as a medical examiner, I haven't said a word, and won't, until after the autopsy. Right?"

"Right."

"You about ready to release the body? I could take it back to Bellevue with me and get right to work."

I gave him a transfer form, waited until he had signed it, and then called to the ambulance attendants who had been waiting just outside with their stretcher.

"See you, Pete," the M.E. said as he followed the attendants through the door. "I'll give you a buzz as soon as I finish."

"Thanks, Ed," I said. "I'll appreciate it." I glanced at my watch. It was a little past ten, on as hot and muggy a New York night as I could remember. I loosened the top button of my shirt, lowered my tie a little, and started down the hallway toward the room where my detective partner, Stan Rayder, was talking with the young girl who had found the body and called the police.

Stan and I had arrived about an hour ago, noted the coal dust on the dead man's clothing and the splintered remains of the plywood cover that had once concealed the basement end of the coal chute, and then had gone out into the alley to check the iron door of the hatch. We'd found that the hatch opened easily, despite the rusty hinges, that the small amount of blood near the hatch meant the dead man had lain in the alley for a few moments while the hatch was being opened, but not necessarily that he had been killed there, and that the hatch was too encrusted with rust and dirt to take any fingerprints, even if the killer had left them. Fingerprints or not, the tech men and the photographer were working out there now, doing the best they could.

Our search of the one-time coal bin had bought us nothing and our search of the body very little more. Someone had removed everything from the pockets of the man's suit, leaving them turned inside out, but had apparently forgotten to look in his shirt pocket, in which we had found an almost illegible phone number scrawled on the margin of a page corner torn from a Manhattan telephone directory.

When I reached the room where Stan Rayder was talking with the girl who'd found the body—her name, she'd told us, was Cloris Ramey—I saw that he had been able to calm her down considerably.

"Feeling a little better now, Miss Ramey?" I asked.

She sat in the exact center of a plum-colored studio couch, her hands folded in her lap and her knees and ankles pressed tightly together, a gaunt, large-boned girl with a small, pale face, an unusually short upper lip, and moist, slightly protuberant gray eyes. She looked at me, nodded, and looked away again.

Stan Rayder had been sitting on the arm of an overstuffed chair opposite her. Now he got up, slipped his notebook into his pocket, and motioned for me to follow him out into the hall. When we were outside, he fumbled a cigarette from the pack in his pocket, lit it, and leaned back against the wall.

"It really hit her," he said. "Let's let her have a few minutes to herself." He looked as if he'd just been mildly surprised by something, an expression which is habitual with him, although he is probably the least easily surprised man I know. The truth is, Stan's whole appearance is deceptive. He's a long, gangling, prematurely gray young man who speaks softly and looks like he might be teaching college math and bucking for a Ph.D. But as many a hardnose hood could tell you, he's got a body like a coiled steel spring and a built-in bomb in either fist.

"She able to add anything?" I asked.

He shook his head. "She thought she heard a sound in there, went down the hall, saw the body on the floor, and called the law. That's her whole story, and I believe it, all the way."

"You check on the other tenants?"

"Nobody else home, Peter. The old couple on the top floor is away for the summer. The two guys on the street floor work nights, and Miss Ramey's father is in the hospital."

"Which leaves us with only a phone number," I said.

"We've started cases with less."

"And got old before our time doing it." I took the page corner with the scrawled phone number from my pocket. "I'm going to find out who goes with this, Stan," I said. "Then—"

"Yeah, I know," Stan said wryly. "Then you're going to leave me here with the dirty dishes while you go off to whoever-it-is's nice, air-conditioned apartment for a pleasant little chat." He shook his head. "It happens every time."

"Not all apartments are air-conditioned, Stan."

"The ones you go to always are. Me, I always end up in a Turkish bath."

I went back into Miss Ramey's room and called the telephone company for a cross-check on the number we'd found in the dead man's shirt pocket. The check took less than a minute, during all of which time Miss Ramey's moist gray eyes never once changed expression, nor, so far as I could tell, even blinked. The name that went with the number was Leda Wallace, 834 West Houston. I wrote the name and address in my book, and put down Miss Ramey's phone number as well.

In the hallway again I told Stan what I'd learned, and then gave him one of the quickie Polaroid shots I'd had the photographer take of the dead man's face.

"I wonder if he ever looked that peaceful when he was alive," Stan said musingly.

"I doubt it," I said. "It's not that kind of world."

"Any special instructions before you leave?"

"No. Just hold down the fort, that's all."

"And sweat myself skinny," he said. "Too bad *I'm* not the one around here who could stand to lose a little weight."

"Just try to rise above it," I said as I headed for the door that led up to the street. "I'll keep in touch."

"You do that, Peter," he said. "Drop me a postcard, now and then."

Eight Thirty-four West Houston turned out to be one of six identical new five-story apartment houses, shoulder to shoulder, an unbroken expanse of bright yellow brick six buildings wide, with nothing to distinguish one from the other except the numerals on the small metal plaques beside the six unornamented entrances.

The girl who answered my ring at the door of apartment 4-B was about twenty, a pale gold blonde with dark-green eyes under tarry-looking lashes and a profile straight off a cameo.

Even in her bare feet, she was very nearly as tall as I was, which made her a pretty tall girl, and the body under the tight jeans and the paint-smeared T-shirt had the completely feminine and yet firm-muscled look of a girl who spends a lot of her time in swimming pools.

"Yes?" she said.

"Miss Wallace?"

"Yes."

I showed her my badge. "Detective Selby, Sixth Squad," I said. "I wonder if I could talk to you."

She started to say something, then changed her mind and stepped back to let me come inside. Because I have to spend so much time on my feet, I sit down every chance I get, asked or unasked. Since she didn't ask, I took a seat at one end of a short, low couch, and got out my notebook and the Polaroid photo of the dead man.

She hesitated for a moment, absently wiping red paint from the back of her right thumb onto the already smeared T-shirt, and then sat down at the other end of the couch and raised one eyebrow about a sixteenth of an inch.

"I hope this isn't going to take long," she said. "I'm really very busy, Mr. Selby."

I smiled, trying to keep it friendly. "Painting your apartment?"

"No. Christmas cards." She gestured toward a cluttered drawing board, tilted up like an easel, in the far corner of the room. "I do them by the gross for this outfit out in Kansas City."

"Painting Christmas cards in August?"

"Yes. And at Christmas time I'll be doing ones for Easter."

"I see," I said, handing her the photograph of the dead man. "We're trying to identify this man, Miss Wallace. Do you know him?"

She took the photograph, glanced at it, and then handed it back to me, dangling it by one corner between thumb and forefinger, as if it had been a dead mouse.

"I know him, all right," she said. "So what has he done this time?"

"It's not so much a question of what he's done as who he is."

"His name's Cody Marden," she said. "Of course, a lot of people call him by *other* names—but after all, there are ladies present."

"No love lost, then?"

"Not a bit," she said, smiling faintly. "Why do you ask?"

"He's been killed, Miss Wallace."

The smile faded from her lips and the green eyes seemed to grow a little darker. "Killed? Cody?"

"He was murdered. By whom, we don't know."

She looked away from me and nodded slowly, as if to herself. "It had to happen," she said. "Sooner or later, it had to."

"Why do you say that, Miss Wallace?"

"Because of the kind of person he was."

"He had a lot of enemies?"

"A lot."

"When was the last time you saw him?"

"About six months ago. Last February sometime."

"And before that?"

"You mean, what kind of a relationship did we have?"

"Yes."

She laughed shortly. "I thought it was, quote, the real thing, end quote. I don't know whether he hypnotized me, or I hypnotized myself, or what. All I know is that I went around for three months in a trance. And then came, again quote, the awakening, end quote."

"About these enemies, now. Any of them enemy enough to want him dead?"

She thought about it. "Well, *wanting* him dead and actually *making* him dead are two different things, of course. When it comes right down to it, I guess the only two people I'm *positive* might kill him would be Fred Bennett and his wife, Joyce. It's been six months since Cody left here, but even so—"

"Left the city, you mean?"

"He must have. Nobody I know of ever saw or heard of him after that. Until you showed up tonight. I didn't know he'd come back. I'm amazed he had the nerve *to* come back."

"This Fred Bennett and his wife," I said. "What makes you think *they* might have killed him?"

"He gave them plenty of reason. Both of them. All the time Cody Marden had me in this trance, he was romancing Joyce on the sly. And then suddenly there's no more Cody Marden *or* Joyce Bennett. They've run off together. And not only that, but Cody's talked Joyce into cleaning out her and Fred's joint bank account."

"And Joyce? What would be her reason?"

"Cody made her the laughingstock of the Village. All Cody'd been after the whole time was that bank account. The minute she turned it over to him, he ditched her and took off for nobody knew where. This was somewhere in Jersey, the way I heard it, and Cody didn't even leave her enough money for a bus ticket back to New York. She had to work a couple of days in a diner, just to get the fare." She paused. "And Joyce Bennett just isn't the kind of person you can do that to. A real primitive type, you know—

all emotion and no thoughts about anything. All you have to do is look at her cross-eyed and she's just as likely as not to explode right in your face."

"She and her husband go back together?"

"No. I hear she wanted to, but Fred told her where to go, how to get there, and how long she should stay."

"You know where Fred's living now?"

"The last I heard, he was at the Merrick, up on 14th Street."

"And Joyce?"

"I don't know. Someone told me she was waiting tables at that new restaurant that opened up where Jody's used to be. You know where I mean?"

I nodded. "We'll need a next-of-kin identification of Marden's body," I said. "He have any family or relatives in New York?"

"No. Not anywhere, so far as I know." She paused. "I just remembered something. Cody had a fight with a man once. An older man. We were walking down the street one night and this man came up and started cursing Cody and calling him a double-crosser and an ingrate, and then he tried to hit Cody. But Cody ducked and hit him instead and knocked him out. Later, Cody said he was somebody he used to work for."

"You don't know who he was?"

"No. It upset me so much that I . . . I recall he was middle-aged and pretty heavy-set, but I don't remember his face at all. Maybe Ralph Tyner would know."

"Who's Ralph Tyner?"

"He used to be Cody's best friend. I guess you might say his only friend. He and Cody worked at the same place for a while."

"You know where I might find Mr. Tyner?"

"Six Eleven Court Street. He has the back basement apartment there."

"I see Mr. Tyner is a friend of yours as well."

"*Used* to be," she said flatly, and let it go at that.

I got to my feet, put my notebook away, and walked to the door. "Pending next-of-kin I.D., we'll need a tentative one," I said. "Would you want to make it for us? It'd be sometime tomorrow morning, probably."

"I wouldn't want to, but I will," she said.

"Good. We'll send a car for you."

"You'll find him, won't you?" she said. "The person who killed him?"

"We'll try, I said.

"I hope you don't," she said. "Whoever it was, he did the world a favor."

Leaving the air-conditioned lobby of Leda Wallace's apartment house for the moist heat of the street was like stepping from a butcher's walk-in refrigerator into a health club's steam room.

I wanted to talk with both Fred and Joyce Bennett as soon as possible, of course, and since the new restaurant where Leda Wallace had just told me Joyce was waiting tables was only two short blocks away, I decided to talk with her first. With the restaurant so near, and parking space in the Village almost nonexistent, I left the department sedan where it was, and walked.

I drew a blank. Joyce hadn't reported for work, and no one at the restaurant knew where she lived. I left one of my cards with a request that she call me, in case she came in later, and then went back to the car and drove up to the Merrick Hotel on 14th Street.

Another blank. Fred Bennett still lived there, I found, but he had left the hotel sometime between six and seven and hadn't returned. I left another of my cards at the desk, got in the car again, and drove to 611 Court Street for a talk with Ralph Tyner, the dead man's one-time best friend and fellow employee.

Six Eleven Court Street was a converted brownstone. In the six-by-six vestibule I found the mailbox with Tyner's name on it, pressed the button beneath it, and waited.

"Who is it?" a man's voice rasped metallically from the grill above the box.

I told him who I was and what I wanted. A moment later the door release buzzed. I walked to the rear stairway, went down to the basement, and walked back to the last door at the rear.

The man standing in the open doorway motioned me inside and gestured toward the nearer of two ancient, ratty-looking overstuffed chairs facing an equally ancient, ratty-looking davenport.

"Better take that one," he said. "The other one's springs have got a life of their own." He was somewhere in his early thirties, with thick black hair so heavily pomaded it looked like wet tar, muddy brown eyes beneath an almost unbroken bar of eyebrow, and a small, blunt nose slightly canted to the left. He sat down on the davenport, pushed his legs out straight in front of him and eyed me expectantly.

"You know a man named Cody Marden, I believe," I said.

"That's right."

"Pretty close friend of yours?"

"I wouldn't say that. I know him. I used to run around with him, off and on."

"Seen him recently?"

"Not for months. Five or six, at least." He paused. "And now let me ask *you* a question. What's this all about?"

"Marden's dead," I said. "Murdered."

The muddy brown eyes narrowed defiantly. "I see," he said. "Then why didn't you say so straight out? Why back into it the way you did?"

"Relax, Mr. Tyner," I said. "This is a homicide investigation. That means asking questions—of you, and maybe a hundred other people. The way a cop asks them is up to the cop. Now, you said you hadn't seen Marden for five or six months. During that time have you heard from him, or heard anything about him?"

He waited just long enough to let me know I couldn't crowd him. Then, "I *heard* from him today. He called me from the airport. Kennedy. The phone was ringing when I got home from work, about a quarter of six."

"What'd he have to say?"

"Not much. He said he'd just got in and that he had to

see me right away. I asked him what about, and he said he couldn't talk about it on the phone. He seemed pretty worked up. Scared or excited or something. He said he was coming right over, and hung up without even saying so long."

"No inkling of any trouble he might have been in or—"

"Nothing but what I told you. He sounded excited, maybe scared."

"I understand you and Marden worked for the same outfit."

"He was there for a few months, about a year ago, but they canned him. Clary Brothers. Wholesale perfume, by the gallon, barrel, or tank car. I'm still there."

"I had a talk with Leda Wallace a little earlier. She—"

"Leda, eh? So *she's* the one that sicked you onto me."

"I started to say she said Cody had a fight with a man he told her he used to work for. It might have been someone from Clary Brothers."

"I doubt it. I'd have heard about it, if it was. I think she must've meant Arther Hill. Cody worked for him a while, too. Cody and Archer had *some* kind of trouble, I know; I didn't know they'd actually had a fight."

"Is Archer Hill a middle-aged man, pretty heavy-set?"

"Yes. I only know him to speak to, though." He leaned forward. "Tell me something, Selby. Did Leda Wallace try nudging you into the idea that *I* had anything to do with what's happened to Cody?"

"No."

"She didn't? I'm surprised she missed the bet. And speaking of fights, did she tell you about the beaut she had with some other girl over Cody? She clobbered the kid right into the hospital."

"She didn't mention it," I said. "What was the other girl's name?"

"I don't know. I'd never seen her before, and Cody said he hadn't either. She was just some kid that Leda caught giving him the eye—and *wham!*, it was call the ambulance. She's got some temper, that Leda. I ought to know—I used to go with her."

"Before Cody moved in?"

"You could put it that way. Actually, he did me a favor. A girl with a temper like that, and as strong as she is . . . Uh, uh. Girls are trouble enough *without* muscles. She's a bomb that walks like a girl, believe me. Like I say, taking her off my hands was a favor."

"That's very interesting."

"She's a very interesting girl. Just don't forget to take along your flak suit."

"Was Marden in any trouble at the time he left here? Trouble that might still have been waiting for him?"

"I've sort of been going over that in my mind. The only thing I can remember is the way he acted once when he got a phone call from somebody named Eddie. I don't know what this Eddie's last name was, but he called Cody one night. Cody was staying with me for a few days while he looked around for another apartment, and this Eddie called one night, about two A.M. I answered the phone, and the guy says he's heard Cody was here and to tell him Eddie wanted to talk to him.

"He had one of these ice-water voices, you know; it'd give you a chill just listening to it. And so Cody says hello, and then he doesn't say another word. He just sits there getting whiter and whiter. Once he *tried* to say something, but he only croaked a little. I wouldn't kid you, the guy was so scared it was all he could do to keep from dropping the phone. And the second he put it down, he tore around here like a madman, getting his stuff together.

"I asked him what the score was, but all he said was that he had to get out of the neighborhood fast and that he'd call me the next day. He didn't, though. I never saw the guy again."

From the room above there was a sudden pounding of heavy feet, and a few seconds later the ceiling seemed to pulsate with the throbbing boom of a string bass.

"Funny, how those bass-fiddle notes come through like that," Tyner said sourly. "That joker upstairs turns on his hi-fi the second he comes in. I'd have moved out, except for my wheel."

"Wheel?"

"Potter's wheel," he said. "That's it over there, beneath that piece of tarp. A basement apartment like this is just about the only place they'll let you have one."

I looked in the direction he'd indicated. The wheel was in an alcove beside the hall door. I hadn't been able to see it when I came in, and I'd had my back to it since I sat down. On the floor around it were two big square cans, one labeled "Plasteline" and the other "White Clay," and two suitcase-sized slabs of clay, variegated from gray to black, like marble.

"A hobby," Tyner said. "It helps me unwind sometimes."

I nodded, stood up, and turned toward the door. "I think that'll be all for now, Mr. Tyner," I said. "Thanks for your help."

I started to open the door, then moved to the right and bent down to take a closer look at the marbled clay. The fresh-earth smell was pleasant, and I reminded myself that I really ought to get out of the city a little oftener. When I turned toward the door again, I almost collided with Tyner, who had come up behind me. His eyes were challenging.

"What's wrong?" he said tightly.

"Nothing," I said, surprised. "What made you think there was?"

He held his expression a moment longer, then laughed shortly and walked back to the davenport. "Just jumpy, I guess," he said. "My nerves have been shot all day. And then hearing about Cody and all . . ." He shrugged apologetically. "Give the wheel a turn or two, if you want to, Selby. Be my guest. Knock out a few pots for your friends, acquaintances, and loved ones."

"Thanks just the same," I said, opening the door. "Maybe another time."

On my way up the stairs I tried to think of some reason for Tyner's strange reaction to my interest in his clay. But I didn't worry it around too long. Maybe, as he'd said, his nerves were shot. And then again, maybe he, like everybody else, had certain areas in which he was just a little nuts.

There were two bars across the street from Tyner's brownstone. I went into one of them and used the phone booth to call Stan Rayder at the scene of the homicide.

"How's it going?" I asked. "You come up with anything?"

"No," Stan said. "In fact, we're buttoning up. I was just putting a police seal on the door when you called. How about you?"

"I'll fill you in at the squad room."

"Good enough. I'm leaving right now."

I walked into the squad room of the Sixth Precinct's station house just as the minute hand on the big electric clock over the wall speaker took the final jerky movement that made it one A.M. Stan Rayder was already at his desk, feet propped up on the edge of his wastebasket, a bottle of Coke in one hand and a candy bar in the other.

"So we meet again," he said as I sat down at my own desk, back to back with his. "I was meaning to save you halfers on this candy bar, Pete, but somehow I made a mistake and ate your half first."

I loosened my tie and reached into the top drawer of my desk for a cigar. "Any action around here?" I asked.

He shook his head, stuck the rest of the candy-bar in his mouth, and chewed thoughtfully with that odd side-to-side jaw motion of his. "No, but give it time. Now how about filling me in?"

I told him about my talks with Leda Wallace and Ralph Tyner and my attempts to see Fred and Joyce Bennett.

When I'd finished, Stan took the final swallow of his Coke, put the bottle on the floor beside the wastebasket, and sighed. "Our dead man seems to have been a real lovable guy," he said. "The question is, how'd he keep from getting dead a lot sooner?"

"He does appear to have had a minor fault or two," I

said. "Do me a favor, Stan? Get a file started on Cody Marden while I see if BCI's got anything on him."

Stan sighed again, took the cover off his junkheap No. 5 Underwood, and reached for a new file folder and a pad of Complaint Report forms. "Always the dirty dishes," he muttered. "Every time."

I called the Bureau of Criminal Information and asked them to let me know what, if anything, they had on Marden. While I waited for them to call back, I glanced through the messages on my call spike, saw there was nothing important, and then started leafing through the arrest flimsies, reports of unusual occurrences, and complaint reports which had accumulated in my In basket, hoping to find some happening in the precinct that might in some way tie in with our homicide.

There wasn't much—the normal number of larcenies and assaults, a couple of narcotics busts, and several family brawls, including one stemming from the theft of a bowling ball by two nine-year-old boys on the sidewalk only half a block from the scene of the murder and which had precipitated a free-for-all by the entire families of both boys over the question of ownership, and still another family squabble half a block away which had ended in trips to the hospital for a man, his wife, and four in-laws. It seemed to have been a fairly slow night; at least there hadn't been anything I could reasonably relate to our homicide.

The phone rang. It was BCI, reporting that they had no arrest record for Cody Marden.

"No file on our boy, Stan," I said as I hung up.

"He's got one now," Stan said, crossing to the file cabinet to put Marden's folder away. "Oh, oh, Pete. We've got company."

I turned my chair to glance toward the counter which runs across the squad room just inside the door. A young woman stood there, looking at me uncertainly.

"Yes, ma'am?" I said. "Maybe we help you?"

"I wanted to see Detective Selby," she said.

I walked over to the counter, pressed the release button

beneath it, and opened the gate. "I'm Detective Selby," I said. "Come in."

Once she'd been beautiful; there wasn't any question about it. Now, there were only traces, memories. The tiny-featured face beneath the blue-black hair had aged too soon, and the wide-set hazel eyes were twenty years older than the twenty years, at most, I was sure she had lived.

"I'm Joyce Bennett," she said in a tired, husky voice as I walked her over to my desk and pulled up a chair for her. "One of the girls over at the restaurant said you wanted to talk to me."

"Oh, yes," I said. "Mrs. Bennett, this is my partner, Detective Rayder."

"Howdy," Stan said, coming around to sit on the edge of my desk so that he could face her.

She nodded to him, crossed her legs, and sat toying with the handle of her large, white handbag. She had the manner of a schoolgirl called to the principal's office for disciplinary action.

"You've heard what happened to Mr. Marden?" I asked.

"Yes," she said tonelessly. "He's been killed."

"More exactly, murdered," I said. "And since we don't know yet who did it, we have to ask a lot of people a lot of questions. We ask everybody pretty much the same questions, Mrs. Bennett, so don't think we're—"

"I'm not a kid, for God's sake," she said sharply, her eyes suddenly ablaze, her voice harsh. "You think I'm simple or something, you've got to talk to me like that?"

The transformation had been so abrupt and so complete that I heard Stan's quick intake of breath. Mrs. Bennett's mouth was twisted now, almost ugly, and I recalled that Leda Wallace had told me she was an emotional type given to exploding in people's faces.

"I was merely—" I began.

"I don't like cops coming around where I work, killing jobs for me, like you done. You wanted to talk with me? All right, so talk."

"Well, to begin with," I said, "when was the last time you saw Mr. Marden?"

"Six or seven months ago. In February."

"Is that when you and Marden were leaving town together, so to speak?"

"I see you've been talking to the right finks. Yeah, we was leaving together 'so to speak.' Only, *he* left for somewhere else and left *me* in Garrensville, New Jersey."

"With you and your husband's bank account?"

"If you know it already, why bother me in the first place?" She gestured toward my cigar. "That thing's making me sick to my stomach."

I put the cigar in the tray and pushed the tray to the far side of the desk. "You ever hear from Marden after that?"

"No. And I didn't want to. You want to know the truth? I'm glad he's dead. I just hope he didn't die too easy."

"And yet, at one time, you felt quite differently."

"At one time, sure. The guy made a fool of me, I admit it."

"You know anyone who might have wanted to kill him?"

"Me for one. Only I didn't."

"Just for the record, where were you, say, from nine to ten tonight?"

"Nine to ten? In my room, up on 10th Street, having a few quiet beers with myself and minding my own business."

"You know a girl named Leda Wallace?"

"A little. A real uppity blonde. Thinks she's an artist. Big deal. The Village is full of them, blondes and artists both." She paused. "Now *there's* the woman you ought to be talking to. She had a thing for Cody like nothing you ever saw. Cody told me all about her, how she was so crazy jealous of him and all. We laughed about it a lot. When she found out about Cody and me, she must've gone straight through the roof."

"You think she might have killed him?"

"Why not? Somebody did. Why not her?"

"You ever hear anyone threaten Mr. Marden? Your husband, for instance?"

"All I ever heard Fred Bennett say in the last six months

is, 'Get lost.' I went crawling back to the guy, but he wouldn't even look at me." She crossed her legs the other way and sat drumming her fingertips on her handbag for a moment. "I mean, who's to blame him? I done him dirtier than any man could take, I admit it. But it was Cody Marden made me do it. It was his fault, the whole thing."

"Did Marden have any acquaintances named Eddie? Somebody he had reason to fear?"

"Eddie? I don't remember him mentioning any Eddie."

"We understand he had a fight with an ex-boss of his," I said. "Would you know anythng about it?"

"I know about *one* fight he had like that," she said. "Archer Hill, the guy's name was. A big-shot art dealer or something like that. He the one you mean?"

"Could be. Do you know what the fight was about?"

"Well, Cody bragged a lot, you know. He was always crowing about how he'd outsmarted somebody, or how he'd done them out of something. Like that. Anyhow, while he was working for this Archer Hill, he found out somehow that the guy was having a couple of other art dealers' phones tapped. So he could know what prices they were getting and who their customers were, you know. That way, he could get the jump on them and steal their customers for himself. And so then Cody went to these other dealers and finked on Hill and charged them for the information. What that did to Hill's business when the news got out was a lousy shame. Cody said it practically ruined him."

"And he bragged to you about this, you say?"

"Yeah, and about how he knocked Hill cold with just one punch. Oh, he was the original sweet thing, Cody Marden was. He was so sweet that every time I think of him I want to throw up." She paused, frowning over at Stan. "What're you looking so surprised about?" she said. "I've been noticing it ever since I got here."

Stan grinned. "I always look this way, Mrs. Bennett."

"Yeah? Well, you ought to do something about it. It makes a person nervous."

"I'll get it fixed first thing in the morning," Stan said,

still grinning. "If not then, I'll do it on my lunch hour."

"Was there anything else you wanted to tell us, Mrs. Bennett?" I asked.

She stared at me sullenly for a moment, and then got to her feet. "Only one thing," she said. "After this, stay away from where I work. It don't look good, and I don't like it even a little bit. Understand? I already got all the troubles I need, and then some."

"We'll try not to bother you any more than we have to."

"Just let me be, that's all," she said, and strode out of the squad room with her shoulders squared and her jaw set hard, ready for anybody or anything.

Stan expelled a long sigh. "My kind of woman exactly," he said. "I wish now I'd saved her your half of my candy bar."

I relighted my cigar, hauled the Manhattan telephone book onto my desk, and turned over to the *H's*. "I've got a strong urge to talk with this Archer Hill, Stan," I said. "After all, he did attack Marden once. Why not again?"

"Why not is right," Stan said. "But me, I'd put my money on Fred Bennett."

I found Archer Hill's number and address, made a note of them, and reached for the phone. The number rang a long time. Then, "Yes?" a man's sleep-blurred voice said irritably. "Who is it?"

"Mr. Hill?" I asked.

"Yes. Who *is* this? Good heavens, man, don't you realize what time it is?"

"Yes, sir, and I'm sorry to trouble you. This is Detective Selby, Sixth Squad. I'd like very much to see you, Mr. Hill."

"At this hour? What on earth about?"

"Cody Marden."

"Marden! What about him?"

"He's been murdered."

It was a full ten seconds before he spoke again, but when he did his voice sounded very much awake. "I see," he said. "Do you have my address?"

"Yes."

"Good. I'll be waiting for you."

Archer Hill was a big man in all directions, an easy two fifty, and he looked even bigger in the awning-striped robe he'd put on over his pajamas. He was in his late fifties, with a round, baby-smooth face, rheumy blue eyes, and a lot of iron-gray hair combed carefully with a wide-tooth comb.

"I put some coffee on," he said as he led Stan and me through his enormous living room to the bar at the far end. "I suppose you boys could use some. I know I could."

Stan and I took stools at the bar while Hill walked around behind it and poured out three cups of coffee. He put cups before Stan and me, sat down behind the bar, and nodded. "All right," he said as he spooned sugar into his cup. "Shoot."

"We understand Cody Marden used to work for you," I said.

"Yes. I'm an art dealer. Cody was my man-of-all-work."

"Seen him recently?"

"No. Not since the first of the year."

"Would that have been the night you had the fight?"

Hill nodded, smiling a little. "So that's it, is it? I was wondering why you'd want to talk to *me* about Cody." His smile widened, but not enough to reach his eyes. "Might one ask if that makes him a suspect?"

"Not necessarily," I said. "We—"

"I understand," Hill said. "As to your question—yes, that was the last time I saw him. A one-punch affair with, unhappily, Cody throwing the punch."

"You home earlier this evening, Mr. Hill?" Stan asked. "Between nine and ten?"

"Yes. I spent the evening with a book." He sat smiling at a point midway between Stan and me. "It would seem that although I am not *necessarily* a suspect, I am a suspect nonetheless."

"Just routine, Mr. Hill," I said. "Was Cody in any trouble that you know of? Any enemies? Anybody threaten him?"

"I never heard anyone actually threaten him, but I do know that two very angry men were extremely anxious to find him."

"Two?"

"Yes. Not together, though. They came separately. They thought Cody still worked for me, you see."

"Who were they?"

"The first to come was a Mr. Bender. No, not Bender. *Bennett*. That's it. Bennett. The other man was someone I should imagine you gentlemen would know much better than I. A loan shark called Denver Eddie. As disagreeable a person as I've ever met, I must say."

Disagreeable was hardly the word for Denver Eddie, I reflected. If he was the "Eddie" whose two-A.M. call had left Cody Marden white-faced and speechless and sent him fleeing from his friend's apartment within minutes after "Eddie" hung up, I could easily understand why. Denver Eddie was vicious, even by loan-shark standards, a muscle-bound sadist well-known on both sides of the law for the pleasure he got from collecting in mayhem what his victims were a bit too slow in repaying in cash.

"We know him," I said. "Cody'd borrowed money from him?"

"I would assume so." He paused. "This other man, this Mr. Bennett, seemed half-crazed. I mean that seriously. I shouldn't be at all surprised if the man were mad."

"And with good reason," Stan said.

"Pardon?" Hill said.

"Nothing," Stan said. "Just thinking out loud."

I finished my coffee and slid off the stool. "Was there anything you'd like to add to what you've told us, Mr. Hill?"

"No, I think not. I only wish I could be of more help."

I put one of my cards on the bar top. "If you do think of anything, give us a call," I said.

"Of course, Mr. Selby," Hill said. "I'll be glad to."

"Ready, Stan?" I asked.

He took the last swallow in his cup, nodded, and stood up. "As always," he said.

When Stan and I reached the street, I went into a sidewalk phone booth and called the squad room to see whether there had been any developments. The detective who answered the phone told me there had been a call for me a few minutes before from a man who had refused to give his name but had left a number for me to call. I dialed the number, and the phone was answered on the first ring.

"This is Detective Selby," I said. "Someone at that number asked me to call."

"Oh yes, Mr. Selby," a man's high-pitched voice said. "This is Phil Joyner. I'm the night clerk at the Hotel Merrick. You were in earlier tonight, asking about one of our guests. Mr. Bennett."

"Yes?"

"Well, Mr. Bennett came in about ten minutes ago. I gave him the card you left for him, but he just glanced at it, laughed and threw it in the sand urn and went on upstairs." He paused. "I just thought you'd like to know."

"Thank you, Mr. Joyner," I said. "We'll be right over."

"I always like to do the police a favor, when I can. A man can't have too many friends, police friends, can he?"

"Better friends than otherwise," I said. "Thanks again."

"Anything new?" Stan asked as I came out of the booth.

"Fred Bennett just got back to his hotel."

"Fine. Let's go welcome him home."

"I think I'll let you do the honors solo," I said. "I want to take a crack at Denver Eddie, and the sooner the better."

"That Shylock's a hard man to find, Pete, even in the daytime."

"Not tonight, he won't be. This is the high-roller night up at Joe Marcy's place on Central Park West. If there are only two people there, Denver Eddie will be one of them. He doesn't play, he just lends money to the losers."

"That's right," Stan said. "I'd forgotten."

"So you hit Fred Bennett, and I'll hit Eddie. Joe Marcy's place is a straight shoot from here on the IND, so I'll take the train, and you can use the car. I can get up there faster on the subway, anyhow.

"What was Bennett's hotel again?"

"The Merrick, on 14th Street."

"I'm on my way," Stan said, turning toward the place where we had left the car. "But watch yourself with that Denver Eddie, Pete. The guy's a psycho."

As it turned out, Stan's warning about Denver Eddie had been wasted. And so had my trip up to 74th Street and Central Park West. Eddie had, for once, failed to show up for the high-stakes poker game. The game was just breaking up when I got there, and none of the players, including a couple of reliable stools, had seen Eddie all night.

As I came out of Joe Marcy's apartment house, I turned right, toward the IND station at 72nd Street, and then, suddenly very tired, I crossed the street and sat down on one of the benches along the street side of the stone wall bordering Central Park. A ten-minute break for a rest and a cigar seemed to be very much in order.

On the next bench, a young couple sat entwined, oblivious to everything, including the fact that the park behind them was a nighttime jungle where cops walked only in pairs, and nervously even then.

I lit a cigar, leaned back, and tried to think of nothing. From beneath the street came a sound like faraway chain thunder—a subway train on its way uptown from the 72nd Street station.

"You hear that rumble?" the young man on the next bench asked his girl friend.

The girl giggled.

"When I was a little kid in Brooklyn," the young man said, "my old man used to tell me it was gnomes down there."

"It was what?" the girl said.

"Gnomes. You know, these little people that live in the ground. He said they had a bowling alley down there, and that's what that sound was—bowling balls rumbling down the alley.

The girl giggled again. "You better get me home," she

said, "or *my* old man will—"

I sat up so straight and so abruptly that the girl broke off and both she and her friend craned around to peer at me.

Good Lord, I thought—*a bowling ball!* The medical examiner had said that Cody Marden's massive skull fracture had been inflicted by something big and heavy and spherical. And what better fitted that description than a bowling ball? Further, there had been a report at the squad room on the theft of a bowling ball on the street only half a block from the converted coal bin where Marden had been murdered, and within minutes of the act.

A stealable bowling ball being at that place at that time could be a coincidence; and then again, it could very well be the murder weapon.

"A nut," the young man on the next bench said as I started off at a fast lope for the subway station. "The lousy town's full of them."

At the squad room I stopped just long enough to pick up the report on the stolen bowling ball, and then I checked out a car and drove over to the headquarters building on Centre Street.

The Lost Property Unit signed the ball over to me and I took it to a desk to examine it, being careful not to add or obliterate any fingerprints. It had been in an old-fashioned round canvas bag with leather handles and grommets, a regulation black ball which hefted like a 16-pounder, showed a lot of use, and had been plugged and rebored. There was no foreign substance on the ball, and only a very small brown stain, which might or might not be blood, on thc bag.

I had meant to trace the ball's ownership by its serial number, from manufacturer through retailer to buyer, but the fact that it had been plugged and rebored would indicate that it had changed hands at least once. Then I noticed the small gilt script—*Fitted by Francini*—stamped between the finger holes, which meant my checkout would be a lot faster and simpler. As a sometime bowler myself, I knew that Francini was a bowling-ball mechanic for one of the city's posh sporting-goods houses. He would have a record of his work, including the name of the person for whom it was done.

I left the ball and bag at the lab for examination, went downstairs, and drove back to the station house. I started up the stairs just as Stan Rayder started down them.

"I hope you had better luck than I did," he said. "Fred Bennett checked out clean. At the time of the murder he was boozing it up in a bar with six friends, and all six of them and two bartenders besides are willing to swear to it." He shrugged fatalistically. "But that's the way it goes in the detective business. How about going down to the Blue Heaven for some coffee, Pete?"

"That, and a couple of country-style breakfasts," I said. "A couple for each of us, that is. We're going to need them."

"Oh? Why so?"

"We've got some very fast, hard work ahead of us, Stan," I said, "and we're going to be at it quite a while."

The work was as hard as I had expected it to be, and took even longer to complete. But, after six hours of it, as we stood waiting at the door of Ralph Tyner's basement apartment, we at least had the satisfaction of knowing that we had done all we could do.

Tyner opened the door, frowned from me to Stan and back at me again, and then silently stepped aside to let us come in. His hair still looked like wet tar, but this time it was uncombed, and the muddy brown eyes beneath their single bar of brow were bloodshot and slightly swollen.

Stan and I sat down on the rat's nest of a davenport and Tyner, after a moment's hesitation, took one of the two battered chairs facing it.

"Well," Tyner said. "More questions, Mr. Selby?"

"A few," I said. "This is my partner, Detective Rayder."

Tyner nodded vaguely at Stan and his frown deepened. "Have you found out who killed Cody yet?" he asked.

"We think so," I said. "We found the murder weapon. A bowling ball. Turns out it was yours."

Tyner laughed, a little hollowly, and not smiling at all. "My ball was stolen weeks ago."

"It was stolen last night," I said. "Minutes after you used it to bash in the back of Cody Marden's head."

He half-rose from his chair. "Are you out of your mind? I did *what?*"

"Stolen by a couple of small boys," I said. "You put it down at the mouth of the alley—why, we don't know yet—and they grabbed it and ran."

Tyner shook his head pityingly. "Man, you *are* out of your mind, aren't you?"

"A bowling ball in its bag, swung by the handle of the bag like a club, makes about as deadly a weapon as—"

"You're off your skull, I tell you!" Tyner said.

"Our lab men found two small pieces of Cody's hair where they'd been caught beneath the leather grommets on the handle of the bag," Stan said.

"Listen—" Tyner began.

"You told Pete you hadn't seen Marden in six months," Stan went on. "But you saw him last night. We know that because we found his fingerprints on a page of your phone book. The same page he tore the corner off of after he wrote down Leda Wallace's phone number. The torn-off corner fits the rest of the page perfectly." He paused. "That puts Marden here in your apartment, Tyner, just before he was murdered."

"You came pawing around in here without a warrant?" Tyner said inanely. "How could you get in?"

"We *had* a warrant," Stan said. "And since you weren't here, we used a piece of celluloid in lieu of a key."

Tyner's lips moved, but he said nothing.

"And still another thing, Tyner," Stan said. "We checked with the people at the house where Cody was killed. We found out that you used to visit a girl there, and that you knew the layout of the basement, and about the coal bin and all. But that was some time ago, and since then the coal bin has been made into a room. You thought you were sending Marden's body down the chute into an unused coal bin, where it'd be a long time before it was discovered. Right?"

Tyner shook his head. His face had the stricken look of a man tearing himself to shreds on the inside while others are doing the same thing to him from without. There are men who can deny their guilt and live with it until their last breath, but Ralph Tyner wasn't one of them. Regret and remorse and plain animal fear were breaking him, and breaking him fast.

"Then, too," Stan said, "we have witnesses."

"Witnesses?" Tyner said thinly. "Witnesses?"

"First, there's those boys who saw you put that ball down at the mouth of the alley," Stan said. "Then there's the bartender at the place right across from the mouth of the alley. He saw the boys pick up the ball, and then a few seconds later he saw you come to the mouth of the alley and look after them, as if you were trying to decide whether or not to chase them. That puts you *and* your murder weapon on the scene at the time of the murder, Tyner. It wraps you up about as good as you'll need to be."

Tyner stared at Stan for long moments; then his gaze lowered to the floor and he sat motionless, staring at nothing.

"As you can see, we know who, where and how, Mr. Tyner," I said gently. "But what we don't know is why."

From somewhere across the city a siren keened, and then died away. Tyner shuddered a little, looking at his hands, breathing shallowly.

"Why did you do it, Mr. Tyner?" I asked.

He took a deep breath and let it out very slowly. "I was desperate for money," he said. "When Cody got here last night he was carrying two suitcases full of ambergris. A little over eighty pounds of it."

"Ambergris?" Stan said.

"It comes from whales," Tyner said. "You find it floating in the sea, or washed up on a beach somewhere. It's very valuable." He seemed to have been seized by a sudden compulsion to talk, as if he'd found an unexpected and welcome catharsis in it. His words now came rapidly, and his face became more animated. "It's used in perfume, to give it diffusiveness and a long life. The eighty-odd pounds Cody had was worth at least $25,000—probably closer to $30,000."

Stan whistled softly.

"It looks and smells like fresh clay," Tyner hurried on. "That's it, over there by the potter's wheel in the alcove He looked at me. "You did think it was clay, didn't you, Mr. Selby?"

I nodded. "And that's why you killed him? For the ambergris?"

"Yes. I work for a perfume company, as I told you last night, and I knew what it was and what it was worth. Cody said he'd shipped as crewman for a shrimper out of Tampa, and that the shrimper captain had found the ambergris in the sand somewhere on the coast of Yucatan. When the shrimper docked in Tampa, Cody waited until the captain had left the boat, and then he emptied his suitcases, put the ambergris in them, and took a cab to the airport. He caught the first plane he could get for New York, and called me the minute he got in."

"Why you?" Stan asked. "Because he wanted a place to hole up?"

"Yes, and because he wanted me to sell the ambergris for him. He knew the Tampa police would have the New York police on the lookout for him. And there were other people here he was afraid of—Fred Bennett and this Eddie I told you about. And since I knew the perfume business and everybody in it, I could take my time and pick a buyer. Cody could pay me a percentage and still make more than he could have on his own."

"You say you were desperate for money?" I said.

"I play the horses. I was in hock to bookies and loan sharks all over town. I was on the hook for over $8,000. It was just a question of days, hours maybe, before somebody's collector worked me over with a club—or worse."

"What happened after Cody made you this proposition?" I asked.

"I told him I'd go along with it, once I was convinced I

was the only person who knew he was in New York. I didn't even know I was planning to kill him until I suddenly realized I was thinking of the best way to do it. Not *whether* to do it, but *how* to do it. But I couldn't think of any way to get rid of his body.

"And then Cody, who'd been drinking ever since he got here, decided he wanted to see Leda Wallace. He said he could get over to her place by using the alleys, where nobody would see him. He tried to call her first, but the operator told him she had a new number, and he wrote it down on a corner he tore off a page in the directory. Then he decided he wouldn't call her after all, that he'd surprise her."

"And you followed him?" I said.

"Yes. I knew the route he'd have to take, and I knew that if I waited until he was almost there, I could kill him without having to worry about what to do with his body. So I got my bowling ball and put on my sneakers and trailed him and when he got to the right spot, I ran up behind him and swung the ball at the back of his head as hard as I could."

"By 'right spot,' do you mean where the coal chute was?"

Tyner nodded. "I wanted to take all his identification and put his body in the chute. But just as I started to open the hatch, I heard footsteps at the end of the alley. I thought someone was turning in, and so I dropped the body and grabbed my bowling ball and ran down to the other end. But nobody came in after all, so I put the ball down in a shadow and went back and finished the job.

"When I got back to the mouth of the alley again, my ball was gone. I looked both ways, and I saw those kids running with it, but they were already half a block away and I was afraid to chase them for fear of calling attention to myself."

"Which would have meant connecting yourself with the murder weapon," Stan said. "Not to mention putting yourself at the scene of the crime at the time it was committed."

"Yes," Tyner said. "When I got home I put the ambergris on the floor there by the potter's wheel, where anyone but an expert would think it was just so much clay, and then I broke up Cody's suitcases and wrapped them in newspapers and put them in a trash basket four blocks from here."

There was a long silence. Ralph Tyner sat quite still, hands palms up in his lap, staring at them with a faintly curious smile, as if he were wondering how such hands could have done the things they had done to Cody Marden.

I glanced at Stan and we got to our feet.

"Ready, Mr. Tyner?" I asked.

He stood up very slowly, his face still set in that small, wondering smile.

"It was all like it was happening in a dream," he said softly. "It still seems like a dream. Even our talking about it like this. Everything. Just like a dream."

It wouldn't seem like a dream to him much longer, I reflected as we moved toward the door. The harsh awakening would come all too soon, and from then on Ralph Tyner's only dream would be a lifelong nightmare.